ADVANCE PRAISE FOR
BLACK WATER RISING

Rayner's characters drive a high-stakes plot. Complete with compelling strengths and flaws, Stanton Frame struggles to find his personal truth while searching for answers about his town. From Angie's fortitude to Jess's fierce commitment, the female characters grab the reader and insist that they, too, must be reckoned with.

> – *Lisa Dalrymple, author of* Double Trouble at the Rooms

Stanton Frame wants to do the right thing. But sometimes "the right thing" isn't clear-cut. In this environmentally charged, edgy drama, when corporate greed threatens his town, Stanton struggles to do the right thing by his girlfriend, his parents, his community, and the environment, but mostly himself.

> – *Dr. Rich Meyrick, author of* Jaspa's Journey

Small town versus big money. Threats of a flood ensure the big personalities rise to the top while others sink, leaving nature to sort it all out. As the rains fall and Black River rises, so do the problems with politics and commitment. Robert Rayner sheds light on the big time issues facing small towns throughout Canada.

> – *Sarah Butland, author of* Blood Day

Just when you think the tension has drawn just about as taut as it can get, the author picks up a six-pound sledgehammer and drives it on home. *Black Water Rising* is a rolling read that will sweep the reader away like a paper boat caught up in a flash flood. You will turn the pages with finger-blistering intensity. This YA novel, guaranteed to entertain and enthrall, is Rayner's best work yet!

> – *Steve Vernon, author of* Sinking Deeper

Robert Rayner writes a stor~~~ ~~~~~~~ ~~~ ~~~ ~~~~ n opposition; it will cause the re~~~~ ~~~~~~~ ~~~~~~ ~ance on the ecological balance o~ ~~~~ ~~~~~ ~~~~~ ~~~~~~ness. The story flows as forcefull~ ~~ ~~~~ ~~~~ ~~~~~~ ~~ the Black River Dam.

> – *Susan White, aut~~~ ~~ ~*he Memory Chair

BLACK
WATER
RISING

ROBERT RAYNER

NIMBUS
PUBLISHING LTD

*The author would like to thank Henry Hatt and
Jim Richard for their advice and guidance.*

Nimbus Publishing Limited
3731 Mackintosh Street, Halifax, NS, B3K 5A5
(902) 455-4286 nimbus.ca

Printed and bound in Canada

NB1195

Cover design: Heather Bryan
Cover photos: Shutterstock
Interior design: Jenn Embree

Library and Archives Canada Cataloguing in Publication

Rayner, Robert, 1946-, author
Black water rising / Robert Rayner.
Issued in print and electronic formats.
ISBN 978-1-77108-443-7 (paperback)
—ISBN 978-1-77108-444-4 (html)
I. Title.

PS8585.A974B53 2016   jC813'.6   C2016-903730-4
                                                C2016-903731-2

Nimbus Publishing acknowledges the financial support for its publishing activities from the Government of Canada through the Canada
Book Fund (CBF) and the Canada Council for the Arts, and from the
Province of Nova Scotia. We are pleased to work in partnership with
the Province of Nova Scotia to develop and promote our creative in-
dustries for the benefit of all Nova Scotians.

For Ben

ONE

Stanton Frame sat up in bed.

Something had woken him. Maybe the lack of rain hammering at the window as it had through the last three days and nights, maybe his father talking on the phone downstairs. But there was something more, a sense of familiarity disturbed. As if the surroundings he'd lived in all his seventeen years were somehow in disequilibrium.

He glanced at his watch. It was 4:00 A.M. on Thursday.

He got up, padded to the window, and looked out at the meadow that extended to the river nearly one kilometre away. Blinked. Reached for his glasses and looked again. The river was gone and the meadow was rippling silver. It lapped at the foot of the oak tree where the swing he'd played on as a child still hung.

The shining meadow disappeared as scudding clouds obscured the moon. Stanton peered into the blackness. The moon reappeared. Now the rippling silver meadow had encircled the oak and was creeping towards the house. His father's voice grew louder. Stanton opened his door a few centimetres so he could see into the hallway downstairs where his father was pacing with the phone as he spoke.

"What the hell do you mean you haven't opened the dam?"

Stanton's mother hovered in the kitchen doorway, alternately wringing her hands and clutching her robe, pulling it tight around herself. The light from the kitchen behind her glinted on her short, coppery hair, making a kind of halo. Even with the backlight, Stanton could see she was frowning and clenching her jaw the way she did when she was seriously worried or upset.

His father growled, "The river may not be over its banks in town but it is out here, and that means in a few hours it'll be over its banks there, too. So call in the crew, Junior, and get the gates open."

Junior Dill was his father's deputy manager at the Black River Power Company. He and Stanton's father did twelve-hour shifts, four days on, four days off. TransNational Power, Black River's parent company, sent managers from the capital, Port Carleton, to cover their time off.

"I don't care what you think," Stanton's father snapped. "If I tell you to open the gates, open them." A pause, then: "Is that so? Then I'll come in and open them myself—and you better not be around when I get there because I'm likely to kick your arse from here to Christmas."

Stanton dressed quickly. Pulling on a sweatshirt as he ran downstairs, he called, "I'll come with you, Dad. I can help with the dam."

His father glanced up and Stanton was struck, as often before, by how much the two of them were alike. They had the same medium height and wiry build, and the same curly, dirty blond hair, his father's tinged with grey. They both wore glasses: Stanton's rectangular, with a hint of green in the frame; his father's round with wire frames, so old-fashioned they were in style again.

His mother said, "No. It's too dangerous."

Stanton groaned. "Mom…."

His father hesitated as he pulled on his rain jacket. "Tell you what you can do, Stanton. Call the gate crew.

2

That'll save me some time. You can use my phone as we drive. The numbers are programmed in it."

His mother started, "But he's got school, and—"

"There won't be any school if the river keeps rising like it is now," Stanton's father interrupted. "Plus the phone's going to start ringing any second and I want you to deal with the calls, please, Angie." The phone rang and he added, "See what I mean?"

As Stanton fetched his jacket from the kitchen, he heard his mother on the phone. "No, the gates aren't open yet, but Willis is on his way in now...Yes, I'm sure he knows the river's in danger of flooding...No, I don't know why the gates weren't opened before now...Yes, I'll tell him."

She hung up and the phone immediately started ringing again. She looked at her husband and rolled her eyes. He bent down—he was half a head taller than her—and kissed her cheek. As she picked up the phone she called, "Be careful, both of you. Stanton, don't go out on the dam—Willis, don't let him—and keep clear of the river."

The car was parked close to the back door. Stanton's father drove carefully on the gravel driveway that led across the meadow to the road.

Stanton looked at the creeping water. "How long before it reaches the house?"

"Depends if the rain's stopped further north and how much rain fell up there that'll drain into the Black River and come down here on top of the six inches we got. And how fast we can get the dam open."

"How come Mr. Dill doesn't have it open already?"

"Says he got a call from head office not to open it and of course, being a good employee, he did what he was told." He looked at Stanton. "That's between you and me. Understand?"

"'Course."

"Anyway, half a day, a day at most, and the river will be all around the house. I may send you back to get your mother out before it's cut off."

"Is she okay on her own with the river rising? Should I stay home?"

His father grinned. "Don't underestimate your mother. She may look and act like she's nervous but she's got more guts than you or me." As he swung the car from the driveway onto the road and accelerated towards Black River, he said, "Get calling now. See who you can raise."

Stanton laid his own phone between the seats as his father handed over his cell. He found the numbers programmed under "Dam." There were eight names. It took four men plus a supervisor, which would be his father, to open the gates.

He was entering the first number when his own phone rang. "That'll be Mom, worrying about me already." He broke off as his call was answered. "Hi, Mr. Hanley. Sorry if I woke you. It's Stanton Frame, calling for Dad...."

His father picked up the other phone. "Angie, for heaven's sake, he's only been gone a few minutes. He's—" He stopped. "Sorry, Jess. I thought you were his mother. He's here in the car, making calls for me."

Stanton started his next call. He was half-listening to his father, who was saying, "They're closed at the moment but—"

Stanton knew why Jessica, his girlfriend of nearly three years, was awake like him in the early hours of the morning. She lived with her grandmother on Musquash Lake, which flowed into the Black River. When the water level in the river was higher than the lake, the flow reversed, and if the level stayed higher in the river for more than a few hours, the lake flooded.

4

He said, "Thanks, Mr. Cuff," and hung up. As he entered the next number he heard his father tell Jessica, "We'll have them open ASAP." He caught Stanton's eye and winked. "Yeah, Jess, I know we get a load of rain every fall and we should have had them open hours ago. Call it a communication breakdown. I can't talk now. I'll get Stanton to call as soon as he's done rounding up a crew for the gates."

Stanton finished his next call. "She's mad, right?"

His father shrugged. "I don't blame her."

Jessica had kept a record of the water level in the lake ever since her parents retired to Florida and she moved in with her grandmother. She accused Stanton's father of keeping the water high on purpose to generate more power. She said he was destroying shore plants and wildlife habitat. Last time she was at the house, she'd told him, "This is the first year there are no loons on the lake, because you've flooded their nests." Stanton had kept quiet, torn between loyalty to his father and his knowledge that Jessica was right. His father hadn't answered, just hung his head and grunted.

They were driving fast, the river on one side, creeping towards the road, woods and fields on the other, interspersed by occasional houses all with their lights on. It was ten kilometres to Black River. The Frames' house and its surrounding meadows was one of a number of old farms strung out along the road between Black River and Big Pond, twenty kilometres farther on. Most of them were no longer farms, their fields grown wild. Stanton glimpsed people at the windows of one house, in the yard of another, peering across the road at the river.

Stanton finished his last call. "They're on the way. Les Cuff and Todd Hanley said they'd been waiting by the phone since last night. Said they nearly called you, wondering why you weren't opening the gates."

He called Jessica. Before he could even say hello, she ripped into him.

"Why didn't your dad have the gates open hours ago?" she demanded.

"Because like he said—" he glanced at his father "—there was some sort of communication breakdown. We'll have the dam open soon, and—"

She cut him off. "No you won't. It takes at least five hours to open it and that's if everything goes smoothly, which it usually doesn't. By then Grandma's house will be flooded and hundreds more nests and plants will be underwater."

"I may have to go back for Mom before the house gets cut off. I could swing around to the lake afterwards, pick you up. We could get a coffee, hang out in town. That's if they start closing roads and school's cancelled."

"It is already. Grandma heard it on the scanner."

"So shall I swing by?"

"I'm not leaving Grandma. But stop in for a coffee if you like. We can watch the cabin get flooded together."

"Promise you won't still be mad because Dad didn't have the gates open sooner."

"I'm mad at Black River Power, not your dad. I just wish he wouldn't always do what the company tells him."

Stanton was tempted to explain that his father was about to act directly against orders not to open the gates, but knew better than to let slip items of company business.

"How high's the water there?" he asked instead.

"If we had a basement it would be flooded already."

Her grandmother's log cabin sat on a rock outcrop, fifty metres from the lake's old high-water level, between twenty and thirty metres from where the dam had kept it for the last few years.

"I could help you move out, if you want."

"We don't want. But thanks. If—when—the cabin floods, we'll move up to the loft. We've got the boat if we need supplies."

"I'll be there as soon as I can, but I'll be busy for a while helping Dad get the dam open."

"Like he should have done days ago."

They were driving fast through the deserted outer streets of Black River. Stanton's father called it an "everything and nothing" town: everything to the people who lived there and whose parents and grandparents had lived there; nothing to the people for whom it was no more than insignificant lettering on a map of the province. He wondered if there was something wrong with his liking the town, while most of his friends claimed they couldn't wait to get away.

They turned onto Riverside Drive, where the lights of nearly all the houses were on and groups of people stood in the street watching the furious, muddy swirl of the Black River. Stanton wondered if they'd been there all night. His father had slowed as he turned onto Riverside, and slowed even more when he turned away from the river and circumvented the green, where the farmers' market was held in the summer, and where a stand of maples, now stripped by the November wind, brought colour and a few tourists in the fall. At the end of the green, which was bordered on one side by the river and on the others by the town hall, the Presbyterian church, and the historical society museum, Stanton's father turned onto Main Street and then onto Mill Street. He drove past the lights of the all-night window at Black River Java and through the gates of Black River Power.

It was four thirty in the morning, and the water was rising.

TWO

There wasn't much to the gravel yard of the Black River Power Company, just space for parking on one side, a storage shed on the other, and the office and the dam straight ahead. The shed was enclosed by a two-metre-high wire mesh fence with rolled barbed wire at the top. Both the gate to the en-closure and the door of the shed were padlocked and both bore signs: *Warning—Explosives* and *Authorized Access Only*. It was where the company stored dynamite to use if an ice jam threatened the dam. Only Stanton's father and Junior Dill were trained to use it, and only they were allowed entry. There was only one key, which Stanton's father kept with him at all times. Every now and then questions would arise at town council meetings over whether it was safe to store dynamite on-site, but he always assured the council the shed was secure and had an alarm. It had never been a problem for as long as anyone could remember.

They drove in through the open gates. The gates could be closed and padlocked but never were because people were coming and going all the time. Someone was always on duty anyway and people from town liked to stroll in and across the yard to watch the river flowing through the dam and to talk to friends working there. Stanton's father parked under a big TransNational Power sign and walked across the lot to where Junior Dill was sitting in his car with the engine running. Stanton followed.

Although the company was owned by TransNational, everyone in town called it Black River Power, or just "the mill." Originally it had been the Black River Pulp and Paper Mill, which operated the dam to provide hydroelectric power for its own saws and grinders. When the pulp mill folded, Black River Power bought it to generate power for the grid, and Black River Power in turn was bought out by TransNational Power.

Junior Dill had deep-set eyes and thick black hair swept back in what seemed to Stanton like an old movie-star style. He was wearing the dark blue suit, red tie, and white shirt he always wore to the mill. Stanton's father was in jeans and a sweater under his rain jacket.

Junior opened his window a crack and said, "I won't be any part of opening the gates. You know as well as I do the last company directive stated the dam was to remain closed, and I told you head office called and repeated the order last night."

Stanton's father leaned close to Junior's window. "And I told you when you took over from me last night that if the river reached a critical level you had my authority to override the company directive and open the gates."

"*You* don't have that authority."

"I do when the idiot telling me what to do is a hundred kilometres away in Port Carleton and I'm standing by the river watching it get close to flood level. Jesus, Junior, we've been watching the river for the last three days talking about when we should open the dam."

"You talked about opening the dam. Not me."

"And you take your orders from me."

"We'll see about that," said Junior, and drove away.

Les Cuff and Todd Hanley, and the other men Stanton had called, had arrived and had been watching the exchange.

Les, who was rangy and tall, his wind- and sun-ravaged face weathered from working at the mill for forty-five years, asked, "What do you want us to do, Willis?"

"Like I said: open the dam."

"Good," said Todd Hanley.

Stanton watched the crew saunter towards the dam, bulky like astronauts in their safety harnesses and survival suits. As if safety harnesses and survival suits would do any good if one of the crew slipped and fell from the dam. Whoever it was would be swept down the falls and through the rocky gorge to where the river mixed with the salt water brought in by the tide from Bonne Bay five kilometres downriver.

He followed his father to the office which perched at the end of the dam, looking down the gorge in one direction, and out to the gates and the road in the other.

"Two jobs for you, Stanton," his father said as he pulled on his survival suit and harness. "While I help the guys, I want you to answer the phone—it'll be people wanting to know the level of the river, why the dam isn't open, is the town going to flood, stuff like that—and every hour or so run across to Black River Java and get a round of coffee."

"Should I tell people we're opening the gates?" Stanton asked.

"Why wouldn't you tell 'em?"

"Thought word would get back to the company, and you'd want to keep it from them."

"They'll know soon enough."

The phone rang as his father hurried out to the dam.

Stanton answered: "Black River Power."

"Why aren't the gates open?" A man's voice, belligerent.

"We're working on them now."

A grunt. Then: "Should've opened them days ago."

The line went dead.

Stanton glanced out at the falls. The men were strung out, working their way along the top of the dam, their safety harnesses clipped to railings behind them. His father was at the end, just setting out. The dam consisted of three iron cradles, each cradle four metres long. The concrete that encased them formed a three-metre-wide platform. Twenty twelve-by-twelve spruce logs stacked one on top of the other in each cradle held back the water.

Les stopped at the near end of the first cradle, Charlie at the far end. The other men, Todd Hanley and Adam Glennie, positioned themselves on each side of a hand crank attached midway to the side of the cradle. At a nod from Stanton's father, Les and Charlie slipped a steel rod with a chain attached down each side of the cradle and twisted the rod so the chain looped around the end of the top log. The chains fed upwards through iron rings attached to a frame that straddled the cradle and from there ran to the winch.

Stanton wondered if they'd like a coffee before they started hauling the logs out of the cradle. He was about to leave when the phone rang again.

"Black River Power."

"Who's this?"

"Stanton Frame."

"Where's your pa?"

"Out on the dam."

"What's he doing?"

"Opening it."

"'Bout fucking time."

The caller, another man, hung up. Stanton left before the phone could ring again. He ran across the yard and out to the road. The light from the all-night window at

Black River Java shone across the sidewalk just thirty metres away. Tess, who'd been one year ahead of Stanton in high school and who now worked full-time at the coffee shop, was on duty. She had wavy blond hair and full lips. She smiled.

"Want to come in? I can open the door."

"Can't. I'm helping Dad."

"Are they opening the gates?"

Stanton nodded.

"Mind if I call my folks and tell them? They've been up the last two nights watching the river."

"Sure. But let me have half a dozen coffees first, for the guys."

He carried the tray of coffees to the dam.

Todd and Adam were winching the first log slowly upwards, while Les and Charlie held the steel rods to make sure the chains didn't slip. Stanton's father had his eyes fixed on the log. As supervisor, his main job was to make sure it stayed level as it moved upwards. If it didn't, at best it would jam against the side of the cradle, at worst, slip from the chains and land at an awkward angle on top of the remaining logs.

He called, "Hold it."

The log was at the top of the cradle. While Todd and Adam held the winch, Les and Charlie hooked peaveys to the log and swung it clear of the cradle.

"Lower it," Stanton's father ordered.

Todd and Adam slowly lowered the huge log to the ground. They slipped the chains off and rolled the log to one side of the dam.

"One up," said Charlie.

"Only fifty-nine to go," Todd added.

It had taken five minutes to remove the first log. In the early days of the dam, three teams had worked at each frame simultaneously, making it a much faster operation.

But when Black River Power had taken over, the company decided that made the platform dangerously crowded, and since then only five were allowed on the dam at one time.

"It'd be a whole lot easier and quicker if TransNational would repair the winch motors so we didn't have to crank the logs up by hand," Les muttered. "Can't you get after them, Willis?"

"I've been after them," said Stanton's father. "But they say it's too old to repair and they don't want to replace it because, like I told you, they plan to update the dam."

Les laughed sarcastically. "Why update it when it's near a hundred years old and the only dam in the country still using this system?"

"They're not going to spend much money on a little operation like Black River," said Todd.

Stanton knew Mr. Hanley was wrong, but didn't say anything. The real reason the company wasn't replacing the motors was because it planned to rebuild the dam as a fully mechanized, computer-controlled operation. The project, which would provide at least twenty jobs for two years but would make the dam crew redundant, was to stay secret until TransNational announced it at a big press conference. His father had told Stanton and his mother, with strict instructions to keep the full extent of the upgrade secret. That was six months ago.

Stanton shouted above the noise of the spray, "Coffee!"

He stood at the end of the dam to pass the coffees out. On one side of him the river roiled against the logs. On the other, there was a nine-metre drop down the falls. He remembered his mother telling him to keep clear of the river. He could understand her concern.

His father took the cups one by one and passed them along the line. The men, soaked with the spray that blew constantly from the falls below, wrapped their hands gratefully around the hot coffee cups. They kept the hoods of their survival suits down so their vision wouldn't be restricted, and their hair was plastered flat across their heads as water dripped from their hair and eyebrows into their coffee as they drank.

At ten o'clock, after Stanton had made three more coffee runs, they'd just finished and were stripping off their safety harnesses and survival suits when two cars pulled in, Junior Dill at the wheel of one. Stanton was passing around coffee and muffins after his latest trip to Black River Java. Junior, tall, leaning, and raw-boned, and still in his dark blue suit, approached with the driver of the other car, a man in khaki slacks, an open-necked shirt, and a battered corduroy jacket.

Stanton remembered Frank Reed from the party TransNational had thrown for his father to celebrate his twentieth anniversary at the mill. Reed was TransNational's provincial manager and he'd made a speech about Willis Frame working for Black River Power and TransNational Power since he was a kid straight from engineering school; the youngest manager ever employed by the company. Reed also wrote a column on bird watching for the *Atlantic Herald*. Stanton read it every week.

Reed strode to Stanton's father and shook his hand. "How're you doing, Willis? How're you coping down here with this shitload of rain we've had?"

"We're coping so far—and we'll continue to cope if the dam's open." He looked hard at Reed and added, "Although I know you've come to tell me to close it."

"I've come to discuss it, Willis," Reed insisted.

"I know the river. These gentlemen do, too." Stanton's father indicated the gate crew. "Unless the gates stay open it's going to flood, like it did five years ago. And the company will be to blame."

Reed held up both hands, shaking his head at the same time. "Whoa, Willis. Let's be careful what we say. Our engineers have determined that the dam staying closed has minimal effect on water levels in the river and the lake. What does have an effect, apart from the rain, is runoff from housing developments with inadequate drainage, like you've got right here in town, and clear-cutting upriver for mile after mile. Jesus, Willis, I've stood up there in the rain and watched it run straight into the river. No one takes any responsibility for that. Meanwhile TransNational has at least studied the problem, and has tried to help people who suffer from flooding—flooding they have no responsibility for!"

"I accept all that, Frank. But—"

"The river and the lake would both have flooded five years ago, regardless, with the amount of rain we had then, on top of all the other factors."

Stanton's father tried to interject. "But—"

Reed held up his hands again and continued, "In other words, if there's another flood, TransNational is not responsible, although of course we'll help the community and flood victims like we did five years ago, and we'll fix any damage done to the environment."

"The computer model Les and I developed using local knowledge predicts that if the dam stays closed the river and the lake will flood," Stanton's father insisted.

"I've seen your model, Willis, and I respect and admire the work you and Les have done on it, but I still have to accept the conclusion of our engineers."

"So let's close the dam," said Junior. "What are we waiting for?"

Reed ignored him. "Come on, Willis. You know the last thing I want is homes damaged and lives disrupted, and I'd certainly never sanction any action by the company that I thought would damage plant or animal life at the lake or on the riverbanks."

Stanton believed Reed. He'd worked for the National Nature Trust and the provincial Conservation Council before he was recruited by TransNational. His father always described him as an honourable man.

"So I hope, Willis, we can agree to disagree about our respective studies, and I also hope we can agree that the gates have to be closed," Reed concluded.

"Sorry, Frank," said Stanton's father. "I don't agree."

Reed took his elbow and steered him a few steps away from the men. Stanton strained to hear.

"In that case, Willis, with regret, I have to overrule you," Reed said quietly. "I'd like you, please, to order the gates closed. You know TransNational doesn't take kindly to its people going against orders. It's likely to lead to dismissal or forced resignation, and then the company has a habit of making it difficult to get another job in the same field in the province. Another thing—" he glanced at Junior "—I don't want to have to ask Junior to give the order. You know he's after your job and would love to see you in shit."

Stanton's father hesitated then murmured, "Under protest...."

"Protest noted," said Reed. "Now why don't we send Stanton for more refreshments while you and I have a chat in the office?"

Stanton's father turned to the gate crew. "Take a break, guys. Thanks again for coming in early."

Reed handed Stanton two $20 bills and said, "Coffee all round, including your dad and me, and yourself, of course, and some doughnuts, muffins, whatever they have."

As Stanton's father and Reed walked towards the office, Junior muttered to Stanton, "Now your dad's going to get his arse kicked."

Reed turned back. "When you've had your coffee, Junior, why don't you go home and get some rest so you're fresh when you take over from Willis tonight?"

"But the gates—"

"Willis and I will take care of everything here, thank you," Reed said firmly.

Junior stalked towards his car.

When Stanton returned with the refreshments, his father and Reed were leaving the office. They shook hands and Reed said, "Good luck with the meeting tonight. There'll be some hostility, some tough questions, but I know you can handle them. Call me in the morning and let me know how it went." He took his coffee from Stanton and left.

"What meeting?" Stanton asked.

"Town council's arranged a public meeting about the flood risk," his father explained. "The mayor asked TransNational to send someone to answer questions. Frank said he'd come but national head office said no and guess who they nominated."

It sounded to Stanton like a set-up. "So you get heat while the TransNational guys making the decisions hide in their offices," he said.

His father muttered, "Something like that." He walked slowly over to the men and said quietly, "I guess we have to close the gates."

Les muttered, "Fucking TransNational."

"But like I told Frank, company regulations say if I can't round up anyone else to take over from you guys—and you know I've called around and can't get anyone...." Stanton's father looked at the crew and added, "Right?"

They grinned, knowing he'd done no such thing, and he went on, "Then you must have at least two hours down time before you work on the gates again. So I'll see you sometime around noon, and I won't be too concerned if you're late getting back."

"I've got a feeling it'll be slow work this afternoon, closing the dam," Charlie said.

"I'm afraid we may not be our usual efficient selves," Adam added.

"So we'll have the gates closed around seven o'clock," said Todd. "Then what?"

"Then we wait for the flood," replied Stanton's father.

"When'll that be, d'you think?" Les asked.

Stanton's father calculated. "Midnight tomorrow."

Stanton looked at his watch: 10:30 A.M.

THREE

It was like driving down the river.

Stanton's father had told him to book two rooms at the Sunshine Motel, the only place to stay in Black River, and then fetch his mother before the house was cut off. As soon as he was out of town Stanton had encountered a police cruiser parked with flashing lights, a barricade across the road behind it. He'd slowed and driven alongside the car. There were only six police at the Black River detachment and he knew them all. Constable Dave Watson, who Stanton's mother said looked about twelve years old with his round, rosy face and thatch of straw-blond hair, was leaning back in his seat with his eyes closed, asleep or dozing. Stanton had driven around the barricade and was accelerating towards a bend in the road when he glanced in the mirror and saw Constable Dave's head jerk up. He'd kept going and rounded the corner so he was out of sight of the cruiser.

And found the river flowing across the road.

How could TransNational say the river wouldn't flood when water was already over the road here? Unless the company didn't count this as flooding—they'd probably blame the low-lying road, saying water often seeped across it in heavy downpours. But this was different.

All he could see ahead of him was water. It was hypnotic, watching it flow. He tried not to look, but it was like driving in a snowstorm, the snow swirling against the windscreen, impossible not to be mesmerized by it. Everything had changed and he couldn't get his bearings, although he'd driven this route hundreds of times. He was afraid of driving off the road. He imagined the car slithering into a ditch and getting stuck, the doors jammed against the sides, trapping him, so he'd have to wait, humiliated, for a tow truck to haul him out. The car crunched into a washout. He slowed, but then was afraid the car would get swamped and the engine would cut out and he'd be stranded—or worse, the car would be swept away with him inside. He could feel the current pulling at it already.

If the car was carried into deep water, would it float for a while, long enough for him to scramble out if he could open a door against the force of water? Or would it sink, so that he sat under water, like in a diving bell? He thought he remembered reading somewhere he was supposed to open a window a crack if that happened, and let the car fill slowly, until he could open the door and slip out and swim to the surface. But the windows were electronic and would be shot under water. And even if he managed to open the door a crack, it would be impossible to hold it there. The force of water would tear it out of his hands, pour in on him, pin him back, trap him until the river filled the car. He pictured himself with his head tipped back, stretching his neck farther and farther, trying to keep his face above water, but the river trickling into his mouth, filling it. Should he spit it out, or swallow until his stomach was full, and it backed up his throat like a blocked toilet? What would it be like, his mouth full of water, unable to breathe? He'd read somewhere it wasn't a bad way to go. But still he wasn't keen to try it.

He was gripping the steering wheel so tightly his knuckles were white. He forced himself to relax. The front wheels slammed into another washout. He swerved, trying to keep the rear wheels out of it, and felt the car leave the pavement. He was bumping along on grass. The car leaned to one side and started to slide. He swung the wheel the other way and gunned the gas. The wheels spun for a few seconds, then the car lurched forwards as he saw the farmhouse ahead. But he couldn't tell where to turn because water covered the driveway across the meadow. Stanton thought of stopping, abandoning the car, and walking to the house, but then he wouldn't be able to get his mother out. He glimpsed the tops of rocks piled years before along the edge of the meadow when the land was cleared. He pictured the gap in the line of rocks where the driveway met the road and lined it up with where he could see gravel emerge from the water near the house.

He swung the car in and found himself bouncing across grass. His mother was at the door, pointing to his right. He turned and felt the wheels grind gravel. He drove out of the river, feeling as if he was driving up a beachhead in a military landing craft.

The house sat on an island like a huge pitcher's mound, the overflowing river parting in front of it, flowing along each side, and joining behind. Stanton remembered his parents talking about how they'd trucked in tons of gravel to create the raised area when they moved back to the house after Stanton's grandfather died. Stanton had been just a toddler then.

His mother smiled. "You made it."

"Just."

She ran to him and hugged him. "I was working at my desk and saw you." She ran a bookkeeping service, keeping accounts for local businesses and organizations. "I watched you cruise up the road. I was afraid you'd be carried into the river."

"Dad sent me to take you to town before the house gets cut off. He couldn't come himself because Junior Dill got Mr. Reed down and he said the dam had to be closed. Dad says now the river will flood at midnight tomorrow."

He followed his mother into the house and came up against a clutter of chairs, tables, lamps, boxes of books, the TV, and stereo, all stacked in the hallway.

"I already got a few pieces upstairs," she said. "You can help me with the rest."

They spent the next hour moving furniture upstairs. When they'd finished, they had coffee by the kitchen window. Watching the water swirling around the house, Stanton's mother said, "The meadow used to flood every spring in your grandfather's time. It was just something that happened every year, an annual event, like Christmas and birthdays and Thanksgiving. It was no big deal, because in those days there was no insulation or Gyproc to get soaked and ruined and go mouldy. We just lived upstairs for a few days, waded through the water downstairs to get out, kept the boat tied by the back door, and waited for the river to go down and the house to dry out. Then your father and I had ditches dug in the meadow and raised the house and we never had a problem—until TransNational took over Black River Power. The company caused the flood five years ago and got away with it. Now they're responsible for the river flooding again. But this time they'll pay for it."

Her voice had grown quiet and she was staring out of the window. Stanton didn't know whether she was talking to him or to herself. He'd never heard her speak so bitterly. She repeated, her voice almost a whisper and her jaw clenched, "One way or another, this time they'll pay."

She shook herself as if coming out of a trance and drained her cup.

The phone rang.

"Hi, Jodie…Just Stanton and me…Hold on. I'll tell him." She rolled her eyes and broke off to tell Stanton, "Your Aunt Jodie says, 'Hi, handsome,' and 'How's Jessica?'"

Stanton liked his Aunt Jodie, who lived alone in Lewisport, a two-hour drive north of Black River. She was a commercial artist who specialized in floral designs. She wore long dresses with floral prints. She always bought old cars because, she said, they were all she could afford. They were always breaking down and never lasted long. Stanton liked teasing her about them. She'd given him an iPad for his last birthday, and with it a year's subscription to Netflix, and always asked him about Jessica. She suffered from something called irritable bowel syndrome that seemed to recur every few months, keeping her in bed for a few days, sometimes sending her to hospital. Stanton didn't like to ask her too many questions about it.

While his mother talked Stanton went up to his room to get some books to take to the hotel. She was still talking when he came back.

"We're moving a bit of furniture before we get flooded again. Then we have to evacuate before the house is cut off…Yeah. All thanks to TransNational…Good idea. Well, why don't you come down and do it yourself?"

When she ended the call Stanton asked, "Come down and do what herself?"

His mother laughed. "Jodie thinks we should dynamite the dam."

Stanton laughed too. "How's she doing?"

"Good. Had a little flare-up last week but she thinks she's got it under control. Come on. Let's get back to town."

"I drove through a police roadblock to get here," Stanton confessed. "I'll get hassled if Dave Watson's still at the barricade."

His mother grinned. "No problem."

She drove fast and confidently, cutting a swath through the rushing water and sending waves surging to both sides of the road. At the bend before the barricade Stanton scrambled into the back and lay on the floor with a blanket from the back seat over him.

He felt the car slow and heard the window slide down and his mother say, "What's up, Dave?"

"Where did you come from, Mrs. Frame? Road's closed."

"Not at our end."

"I guess Highways hasn't got around to putting up the barrier there yet."

"No problem. It's not too bad."

"Did Stanton drive this way earlier?"

"No. Why d'you ask?"

"Someone drove past the barrier a couple of hours ago."

"Car's been parked at home since I drove Willis in early," Stanton's mother lied. "Only reason it's out now is I want to see what's going on with the dam."

"Tell Mr. Frame to open it wide and keep it open, eh? Black River doesn't need another flood."

Stanton, still under the blanket, thought, *But you're going to get one.*

In about thirty-five hours.

FOUR

Stanton groaned, "Not again."

He stopped the car. It was two o'clock and he was on his way to the cabin on Musquash Lake where Jessica lived with her grandmother, Lily Caithness. There was a police roadblock just before the narrow, winding road ended in a boat launch at the lake.

Sergeant Ernie Munn, the Black River police chief, strolled to Stanton's window. He had a round, florid face crowned with thick, wavy white hair that made his cap look too small for his head. "Water's creeping over the road ahead," he said. "It's already halfway up the boat launch. Don't want anyone driving into the lake."

Stanton nodded. It happened several times a year, drivers taking the last bend too fast and ending up at the bottom of the ramp, water up to the windows.

"I'm guessing you're on your way to see Jessica at her grandma's," Sergeant Munn went on. "Why don't you leave the car here? I'll keep an eye on it."

Stanton thanked him and pulled onto the grass at the side of the road. He walked down to the flooded boat ramp and looked to his right, where Musquash Lake flowed into the short natural canal that linked it with the Black River. The water seemed to be in temporary equilibrium. It wouldn't last. When he'd dropped his mother at the mill, from where she said she'd walk to the hotel, the gate crew already had one cradle of the dam closed. When they finished, it wouldn't be long before the river started flowing into the lake, flooding it and the cabins around it.

Stanton set off on an old woods road that branched to the left of the boat launch, glimpsing the lake through the trees as he walked. After half a kilometre he turned onto a trail that rose through the woods before emerging on a rocky bluff that looked across the lake. Lily Caithness's cabin stood at the highest point of the bluff. The water lapped only a few metres from it. After the flood five years ago she'd had to move out for two weeks while repairs were carried out.

He walked to the front of the cabin and peered through the open door into a room that was living space, dining room, and kitchen. A curtained area in one corner served as Mrs. Caithness's bedroom. Jessica was struggling up the ladder to the loft, a box of books under one arm.

She turned to look down at him, her hair, the colour of the coffee Tess served at Black River Java, framing her wind- and sun-tanned face.

"Can't you get your dad to open the gates?" she greeted him. She was wearing black tights under a short, moss-green skirt, and a navy sweatshirt he'd loaned her a year ago and told her she could keep. He liked the idea of it lying next to her skin.

"They are open," said Stanton.

It wasn't a *total* lie.

"He should have opened them before. He knew how much rain was coming."

Stanton didn't answer. There was no point. Jessica would hold his father personally responsible for the opening and closing of the dam whatever he said, even though he'd pointed out over and over again that his father had to do whatever head office told him.

"I just came to help move stuff," said Stanton.

Jessica's grandmother appeared from behind the curtain in the corner, sheets, blankets, and pillows piled in her arms. She was lean and small, a head shorter than Jessica. Her movements were quick and darting, as if she had a task that had to be accomplished immediately, however inconsequential. She'd grown up in the cabin and, after inheriting it from her parents, had used it as a weekend retreat while she and her husband lived and worked in Montreal. She'd retired to the cabin when she became a widow.

She smiled and said, "Hi, Stanton."

He took the bedding from her and followed Jessica up the ladder to the loft. It was packed with boxes, rugs, and chairs, crowding the low, narrow cot where Jessica slept. She took Stanton's hand and pulled him to her. She kissed him and said, "Thanks for coming." Then she added, grinning as she pointed at a makeshift bed of blankets and cushions beside her cot, "Grandma's sleeping up here with me. Don't expect much action if you're planning on staying the night."

They spent half an hour cramming more furniture and furnishings into the loft before Mrs. Caithness said, "That's all we can do. I'll put the kettle on."

They had tea sitting on the floor, looking through the still-open door at the lake. Stanton was about to leave when Mrs. Caithness's neighbour, Fred Shingles, stalked in. He had staring eyes and wispy white hair that sprang in tufts from his head, and wore grease-stained jeans and a checked woollen jacket with a tear in one arm. Stanton reckoned he was in his eighties, at least ten years older than Jessica's grandmother.

"Don't bother to knock, Fred," said Mrs. Caithness. "What can I do for you?"

"Nothing. You need anything?" He spoke gruffly.

"No."

"Good. That's what I came to ask."

His cabin was on the other side of the bluff. It was even smaller than Mrs. Caithness's, and was on lower ground. It would be the first to flood.

He marched across the room, leaned down, and put his face close to Stanton's, his arms back and his neck thrust forward like an angry goose. "I'll sue your father if I get flooded again."

"It wasn't Dad's fault the river flooded five years ago and it won't be his fault if it floods this time," Stanton retorted, trying not to recoil from Shingles's fishy breath.

"You should work for TransNational, like your old man," Shingles sneered. "You talk like one of their guys."

"That's enough, Fred," said Mrs. Caithness. She stood and took his arm gently, pulling him away from Stanton. "It's not all TransNational's fault the water's so high. It's 'cause of weather patterns changing, too. You've talked about that yourself; how we're getting our rain all at once, not spread over the year like when we were kids."

"It's companies like TransNational and people like Willis Frame causing that, too. And getting away with it. They're burning up the ozone so we got oceans rising, glaciers melting…."

"But it's not just companies like TransNational causing all that," Stanton protested.

Jessica caught his eye and shook her head. Stanton shrugged. He knew it would be better not to respond, as Jessica was indicating, and he knew what Shingles said about climate change was true, but he had to defend his father.

Shingles turned on him, talking faster, leaning forward again, while Mrs. Caithness still held one arm.

"TransNational and your dad manufacture the power that's destroying us, and they manufacture it by playing God with the water levels in our river and lake. I worked for Black River Power so I know all about the company and how it works the dam."

Jessica jumped up and took Shingles's other arm. "Relax, Fred. Why don't you sit with us and I'll pour you some tea?"

He shook himself free and stared across the lake as he murmured, "More rain, less snow. More wind, less calm. More sun, less cloud. No winter. No spring. No summer. No fall."

It was like an incantation.

"Come on, Fred," said Mrs. Caithness. "You can't have no seasons."

"You can when they're all the same. One unending heat wave burning us up. Wind blasting our skin raw."

"Let's get you home," said Jessica. "I know you don't have a loft, but Stanton and me could help you drag stuff outside to higher ground, cover it with a tarp…."

"Nah. If it floods, it floods. Nothing I can do about it. But TransNational will pay this time. Yessir, one way or another, TransNational will pay this time."

Stanton looked sharply at him, thinking of his mother gazing through the window at the advancing water and saying almost exactly the same words.

"I got friends who'll supply me with what I need to take care of TransNational," Shingles went on. "Saw them a few weeks ago. They know how to make companies like TransNational pay."

"We all know about your survivalist club, Fred," said Mrs. Caithness, soothingly. "It's nice you've got friends to go camping with."

"Not camping," said Shingles. "Training."

She pushed him gently outside, saying, "Jessica and Stanton will get you home and you tell them if there's anything they can do to help. And stop your threatening talk or you know that sooner or later Sergeant Munn's going to hear about it and he'll be paying you a call."

Jessica took one of Shingles's arms and gestured to Stanton to take the other and they walked him slowly across the bluff. When they reached the cabin Shingles fumbled in his pockets and produced a key. Stanton was surprised. Most people in Black River weren't too bothered with security. Mrs. Caithness didn't even have a lock on her door. He followed Shingles and Jessica inside. It was his first time in the cabin. He stopped and stared.

There was no window; the only light came from the open door. The walls were lined with shelves stacked with canned and dried food: beans, tomatoes, vegetables, soup, spaghetti. A sleeping bag, a pillow, and a pile of blankets lay against the back wall. At least a dozen big plastic jugs of water stood in one corner. A wood stove with a steaming kettle on it sat in another corner. Saucepans and frying pans hung on the wall behind, and firewood was piled neatly on each side. Stanton reckoned that made at least five cords together with the tarpaulin-covered stack he'd seen outside. The only furniture in the cabin, apart from a rickety chair, was a table.

Two shotguns lay on it, and a box under it with the label *Danger: Explosives.*

"Are you sure we can't do anything to help?" Jessica asked.

Shingles grunted. Stanton was still staring at the table. Jessica nudged him and nodded towards the door.

As they walked back across the bluff, Stanton said, "Did you see what he had in there? It looked like he was ready for a war."

"He's had guns and supplies at the cabin as long as I can remember. It's just his way. He thinks some kind of Armageddon's going to happen and he wants to be ready for it. He talks about it all the time."

"But…explosives?"

"That's something new," she admitted.

"Should we tell the police?"

"No need. Sergeant Munn knows about him and keeps an eye on him. He calls in with a coffee and pastries for him at least once a month. They'll sit on the rocks and talk for hours in the summer. Fred's harmless."

Stanton muttered, "If you say so."

"Can you pick me up for the meeting tonight, if your folks don't need the car?" Jessica asked.

Stanton had forgotten about the town meeting. Being with Jessica had that effect on him. "Sure."

"I have to be there early. I'm meeting a couple of people from a BC environmental organization."

"BC—as in British Columbia? And they're sending people right across the country for a meeting in Black River? How do they even know Black River exists?"

"I tweeted about how TransNational was fooling around with the water level and damaging the lake and the river, and EcoAction—that's the name of the organization—started following me. When I posted about the flood, I got a tweet saying a couple of people were on the way to help protest against what the company's doing. They want to help us. They've got cells—"

"*Cells?*"

It made them sound like revolutionaries, or an underground resistance movement.

"Yeah. Cells—like, little groups—all over the country, and in the States. We're the Black River Cell."

"We? Like—who?"

"Me and you. And Fred. You need at least three members to be a cell." She went on, talking quickly, "I was going to ask you, but I knew you wouldn't mind, seeing as you're concerned about the environment, like me." She kissed him quickly and lightly on the lips. "After all, it's what got us together in the first place, remember?"

Stanton nodded, recalling the summer his parents had bought him a canoe and he'd started exploring up the Black River to the lake. He'd seen Jessica swimming from the rocks in front of her grandmother's cabin. It was her first summer at the lake. Stanton had ventured back several times, paddling closer each time, until one day she'd shouted, "What are you looking at?"

They'd spent that summer exploring the lake in their canoes. She'd led him to the northern end and said, "Tell me what plants you see growing along the shore."

"I don't see any," he'd confessed.

"Grandma says the shore was lined with thousands of sweet flags and marsh marigolds and water plantains until just a few years ago. Then TransNational started monkeying around with the water level and the plants disappeared. Next thing, the beavers and otters moved out because they couldn't find enough to eat."

"My dad works for the power company," Stanton had said, a bit sheepishly.

She'd responded, "I know who you are."

He hadn't known whether to be flattered or apprehensive.

They'd walked along a beach on the western side of the lake, holding hands until they heard a loud, whooping call and she'd pointed to a lone bird swimming and diving a few metres from shore.

"A red-necked grebe," she'd murmured. "It might be the last one left on the lake."

"How come?" he'd asked, although he could guess the answer.

"The power company keeps the water level so high they've lost their nesting ground."

"Like the loon," he'd ventured.

She'd rewarded him with a smile. "You're learning."

She planned to study ecological restoration and political ecology at the University of Victoria's School of Environmental Studies. She was only a year younger than him, only a grade below in both elementary and high school, but he'd never noticed her before then. Now he couldn't take his eyes off her when they were together, and when they were apart her image flooded his thoughts.

Stanton snapped out of his reverie when Jessica said, "Don't worry. The EcoAction people are coming to help us, not stir up trouble."

"Who said anything about worrying?" said Stanton, trying not to worry.

Back in town at five o'clock, he found his father still at work on the gates while his mother was reading a magazine in the office. She told him they were going straight to the community centre for the meeting and they'd get something to eat on the way. They'd walk, so he could take the car. She said, "See you at seven."

About the same time as the gates are closed. That'll go over well at the meeting, Stanton thought.

At the hotel, he googled EcoAction. Hundreds of references came up.

He clicked on the first and found a headline from the *Toronto Star*: "Canadian Environmental Organization Suspect in Threat to Bomb Keystone Pipeline." The story went on: *EcoAction, based in Vancouver, BC, has been named by police as the chief suspect in an anonymous threat to blow up sections of the Keystone pipeline.*

Stanton clicked on another site and read a report from the *Globe and Mail*:

> *Police, politicians, and oil executives are criticizing an online game developed and posted on YouTube by BC-based environmental organization EcoAction. The game involves a number of tasks to be accomplished on the way to successfully bombing a gas pipeline. A spokesman for EcoAction who wished to remain anonymous said, "It's just a game. If people take it seriously, and use it as a kind of instruction video on how to make a bomb and blow up a pipeline, we can't be held responsible for that, any more than the makers of* Grand Theft Auto *can be held responsible for an increase in car thefts."*

Stanton found another article, this one in the *Alberta Review*:

> *A bus full of oil workers was held up at gunpoint on its way to a work site in the oil sands. The workers were ordered out and the bus hijacked. By the time police found it, it was a few kilometres away and nothing but a burnt shell. EcoAction, whose members have been demonstrating against the oil sands project, denied responsibility.*

Stanton then skimmed through a CBC report from a year ago:

Anti-fracking demonstration turns violent in Manitoba…Demonstrators threw rocks and Molotov cocktails at police…Three officers injured and two police cars set on fire…Police spokeswoman Sergeant Marcia Dunn said: "Outsiders have infiltrated the local protest group and are using it for their own anti-government and anti-development agenda." When asked who the outsiders were, she said, "Members of EcoAction."

One last report caught Stanton's eye:

An explosion last night rocked the community of Wood River, Nebraska (population 850), partly destroying a hydroelectric dam still under construction. When completed, the project will result in 2,000 acres of farmland lying under water. A police spokesman, Sergeant Clyde Herriot, said: "We know EcoAction has the knowledge and the means to blow up a structure such as this. Make no mistake, this is a terrorist organization."

Stanton shut off the computer and sat back in his chair, wondering what Jessica had got herself into.

FIVE

"So why are you worried about EcoAction?" Jessica asked.

It was six thirty, less than thirty hours until the river flooded. They were driving into town for the meeting. She was sitting close to him, her hand resting on his knee as he drove. They'd parked by the lake for a while before setting off. She'd come to the boat slip at the end of the lake road in Mrs. Caithness's aluminum boat because she thought the woods road was about to flood and then the only way to and from the cabin would be by water.

"Just, it looks a bit extremist," he said cautiously.

"Like it takes action against companies that are ruining the environment," said Jessica.

"Extreme action."

He'd nearly told his father about EcoAction. In the end, though, he hadn't. While not telling would be a kind of betrayal of his father, telling would be a bigger betrayal of Jessica. He liked to think they told each other everything, about their feelings, families, ambitions, and fears. If he blabbed about EcoAction, would she ever confide in him again? Besides, if he told his father, what could he do? Have Sergeant Munn stop the EcoAction people at town limits, or run them out of town?

"Extreme action's all that works sometimes," said Jessica.

She withdrew her hand and moved away from him. He wished he'd never mentioned googling EcoAction.

"But…blowing up dams and pipelines, holding up a bus, damaging property…."

"Boo-hoo."

"And risking people getting hurt. It's like doing something as wrong as what you're demonstrating against."

"So what would you do if a company ignored your protests, or, worse, set the police on you?"

"I don't know, but it wouldn't be something like that. Like, you know, direct action."

"Not even if it's to fight against something you know is wrong, and you've tried everything and no one will listen, and it's the only thing left to do?"

He shrugged. "I suppose then I might."

"Just—you *suppose* you *might*," she scoffed.

They'd never argued like this before. They drove the rest of the way in silence.

The Black River Community Centre was on Main Street, between the Baptist church and the liquor store, and opposite the Anglican church and Carmichael's Country Diner. A two-storey brick building, it had been the elementary school until a new K-12 campus was built on the edge of town. Every time Stanton entered he was sure he could smell wet coats and washrooms.

It was easy to pick out Jessica's contacts from EcoAction. The two young women, only a few years older than her, were the only strangers among the crowd on the sidewalk in front of the hall.

Jessica said, "You're from EcoAction—right? I'm Jessica Frith."

One of them, offering her hand, said, "Callie Jost."

Her pale green shirt was open at the neck, revealing a beaded necklace, and she wore tight black jeans and heavy hiking or climbing boots. She had black hair cut short and spiky, and silver framed-glasses with narrow lenses.

She looked at Stanton. "Who's this?"

She didn't offer her hand.

"Friend," said Jessica.

Not "boyfriend," Stanton noted. Were boyfriends not allowed in EcoAction cells?

"Stanton Frame," he said.

The young women from EcoAction exchanged a glance.

Callie Jost looked back at Stanton. "Your father runs the dam."

Stanton looked at Jessica.

She shrugged. "I gave EcoAction some background."

Callie glanced at Jessica. "Whose side is he on?"

"Ours," said Jessica.

Callie looked hard at Stanton. "You better be."

Jessica held her hand out to the other girl. "Hi. I'm Jessica."

Callie's companion ignored her. Her blond hair was short at the sides but long at the front, so it fell like a fan across her forehead, ending in a point just above one of her blue eyes. She was taller than Callie, and wore a loose black T-shirt and a short black skirt. Her long, bare legs ended incongruously in heavy boots like Callie's.

"This is Brynne Tanner. She doesn't say much," Callie said. She grinned at Brynne. "Do you, Brynne?"

Brynne grunted, unsmiling.

They both had bulging backpacks at their feet.

"Why don't you leave your bags in the car?" said Stanton. He moved to pick them up but the girls seized them before he reached them. He led the way to the car and opened the trunk. The girls swung the bags in. They landed with a metallic *clunk*, as if tins or canisters were banging together inside.

"You don't travel light," Stanton said.

"We're ready for anything," said Callie.

As they made their way inside, Stanton caught snatches of conversation:

"…heard Frame's closed the gates…"

"…can't face being flooded again."

"…company doesn't care about us…"

"…neither does Frame…"

They found seats near the back of the hall. Stanton looked around. His father sat behind a long table at the front, facing the crowd. He was alternately clenching and stretching his hands. He did it when he was nervous. The mayor, Verna Mullen, a large woman with close-set eyes, thick lips, and a mass of grey-black hair, sat beside him. She was a lawyer and had run unsuccessfully in the last provincial election. She planned to try again in the next. Stanton's mother sat in the front row, next to Les Cuff, Todd Hanley, and the rest of the gate crew. Stanton saw several other mill workers among the crowd. Tess from Black River Java, sitting with her father, waved at him.

Fred Shingles leaned against the wall at the back of the room, glowering around. Sergeant Munn stood nearby, constantly scanning the crowd. Stanton saw his eyes settle on Callie and Brynne, and he wrote in a small notebook. He looked up, caught Stanton's eye, looked at Callie and Brynne, and back at Stanton. He raised his eyebrows in an unspoken question.

Or warning.

At seven o'clock Verna Mullen welcomed the crowd. She said the meeting was to give townspeople the opportunity to question TransNational Power about the operation of the dam, and for TransNational to allay fears of flooding.

"I know you are all anxious about the level of water in the river and lake—"

Someone called out, "Caused by TransNational."

It was Fred Shingles.

"And you all remember the flood of five years ago—"

"Caused by TransNational."

Fred Shingles again.

Someone else added, "You bet we remember."

Verna Mullen pressed on. "Let's also remember TransNational's generosity at that time, and how the company helped the town clean up after the flood, and the donations they made to people in distress—"

"Guilt money," Shingles shouted. "Cheap way of buying people off."

Sergeant Munn caught Shingles's eye and put his finger to his lips.

"And what an important role TransNational plays in the economy of our community," Verna Mullen continued. "We hoped head office would send someone from senior management to address you tonight but the company declined and instead nominated our local manager, Mr. Willis Frame."

Stanton hated the mayor for her careless put-down of his father, who stood but kept his eyes on the table in front of him. Stanton watched him twice clench and unclench his hands. He wished his father was a salesman at Sears, or a farmer, or a lineman, or a taxi driver—anything that would afford him anonymity. He shouldn't be exposed to such thoughtless criticism from people who didn't know, let alone understand, how torn up he was over the decision; how it wasn't really his, but imposed by distant and uncaring senior management.

"Lost your voice, Willis?" a woman shouted.

"He's afraid to say what TransNational told him to say," another woman taunted.

Stanton's father lifted his head. He smiled at his wife, nodded to Les Cuff and the crew, thanked Mayor Mullen for her kind introduction, and looked around at the crowd. "I don't blame you for being upset," he started. "I don't know what I can say to lessen your worry."

"You can start by saying the dam's open," Fred Shingles called out.

Stanton's father ignored him and went on, "I can say that Black River Power has always tried to keep a balance between using the river to generate power and bring employment and prosperity to the town, and letting it flow as naturally and safely as possible."

"That may have been true for Black River Power," someone shouted, "but you're not Black River Power, not anymore. You're TransNational, and that's another story."

"The policy didn't change when TransNational took over," Stanton's father insisted.

"Like hell it didn't," the heckler retorted. "The water in the river and the lake never used to be this high."

"What's more important, Willis? Making money for TransNational or keeping the town safe from flooding?" someone else called out.

"Don't forget that when TransNational makes money, the town makes money, too," Charlie Hatt retorted.

For a few seconds individual voices were lost as people turned on one another, some supporting the mill, some against it.

Then Fred Shingles's voice cut through the commotion. "I've got one simple question for Mr. Frame."

"Go ahead, Mr. Shingles," said Stanton's father.

"Is the dam open?"

"Before I answer that, let me point out that a study—"

"Is the dam open?" Shingles repeated.

"Let me finish, please," said Stanton's father. "A study by our engineers shows that whether the dam is open or closed makes little or no difference to water levels in the river and the lake."

"To hell with your engineers' study," said Shingles. "Just answer the question, Frame. Right now—is the freakin' dam open or closed?"

Sergeant Munn said sharply, "Watch it, Fred."

Stanton's father hesitated. "It's closed."

A barrage of shouts erupted from the crowd.

"Why?"

"Then you better open it—or else...."

"You don't learn, do you?"

"You just don't care...."

Stanton wanted his father to say he'd closed the dam only when Frank Reed overruled him. If he'd refused, Stanton had no doubt he would have had to quit or be fired. He would have been proud of his father if he'd quit, but he knew why he didn't. He'd heard his parents discussing their finances often enough. His father stayed at the mill so they could pay for Stanton to study engineering, like his father.

So what was best? Compromise your beliefs and principles and jeopardize a community in order to look after your family? Or stick to your beliefs, make yourself a proud martyr, and to hell with your family?

His father started, "Keeping the dam closed is a difficult decision—"

A woman interrupted. "All you're interested in is making money."

Todd Hanley turned in his seat to face her. "Do you use power?"

"Of course I do, but—"

"So where the hell do you think it comes from?"

Stanton's father tried again. "If the river floods, it will not be TransNational's fault, but the company will offer financial assistance to anyone who suffers flood damage, just like it did five years ago."

There was an outburst of jeers and a few boos from the audience.

Les Cuff stood and surveyed the audience, which slowly grew quiet. "Let's remember, folks, TransNational employs over thirty people in good-paying jobs the town badly needs. That's thirty people who spend their wages here in Black River at SaveEasy and Foodmart and Home Hardware and Black River Java and Pharmasave and all the other stores. Black River needs TransNational Power. Suppose there was no dam and no TransNational—"

"Sounds good to me," someone shouted.

"Then there'd be less work in town, which'd mean less kids in our school, which would mean less teachers and probably more split classes," Les went on. "There'd be less stores, probably no post office, and less money for the town to spend on recreation and beautification and summer festivals."

"Don't forget the computers we gave the high school," one of the mill workers called.

"And we paid for lights at the ball field," another added.

"Who needs all that stuff?" Shingles scoffed.

Les looked around at the audience again. "Raise your hand if you think it's good that we've got all that stuff in Black River for our kids and ourselves."

Most people in the audience slowly raised their hands, sneaking sideways looks at their neighbours as they did.

Les grinned. "You might not want them, Fred. But seems most folks do."

He sat down, and a hubbub of discussion spread through the audience, until Verna Mullen stood and announced, "At this point, I think it might be useful for us to hear a history of the dam, so we have a full picture of the events that have led to where we are today, and of Black River's relationship with the dam and with the companies that have operated it. Mr. Frame, maybe you could start with its construction in 1899."

Callie muttered to Stanton, "Your old man's giving us a history lesson?"

"Sorry," said Stanton.

"Let's get out of here," she said.

SIX

Callie, Brynne, Stanton, and Jessica slipped outside. Callie led the
group to a patch of darkness beyond the lights of the hall.

"Where's the dam?" she asked.

Stanton pointed along Main Street. "Few minutes' walk.
Turn left down there onto Mill Street."

"What kind of security?"

"One person in the office. That's about it."

Was he betraying his father by telling Callie this? It was
common knowledge, nothing she couldn't easily discover
for herself.

Callie looked at Brynne. She nodded, and they set off at a
trot. Stanton and Jessica followed. There was no one around.
It seemed the whole town was at the meeting. They turned
onto Mill Street and were passing Black River Java, Black
River Power just ahead, when Brynne suddenly veered
into the coffee shop's empty drive-through and crouched
in the darkness against the wall. Callie did the same. Stanton
and Jessica hesitated. Callie grabbed them and pulled them
down. A few seconds later Sergeant Munn drove slowly
past, peering around.

"Is he following us?" said Stanton.

"What d'you think, dickhead?" said Callie.

They watched him turn into Black River Power and
make a slow circuit of the yard. He drove out onto the
road and turned towards them. Brynne scurried across the

still-deserted drive-through and pressed herself against the wall on the other side so the car's headlights didn't catch her. The others followed. Sergeant Munn drove slowly past again, still looking around. He stopped at the junction with Main.

Brynne waited until he pulled out and drove on. Then she led the way to the gates of Black River Power. She stopped in the darkness beside the light flooding from the yard and asked Stanton, "Where's the office with the guy on duty?"

Her voice was a low, murmured drawl. Stanton had to strain to hear her.

"Straight across the yard."

"And the dam?"

"Other side of the office."

"Can you see the dam from it?"

"Looks down on it."

"How much can you see?"

"Everything. It's floodlit."

"You and Jessica stay here and keep out of sight. You ready, Cal?"

Callie nodded. Brynne stumbled out in front of the gates.

Callie went after her and screamed, "You bitch!"

She grabbed Brynne by the shoulder and spun her round. She pushed her with both hands, sending her stumbling backwards into the yard.

Callie marched after her and pushed her again and screeched, "Fucking slut!"

She slapped Brynne across the face. Brynne reeled back and fell to her knees. Stanton, peering through the chain link fence that surrounded the yard, saw the office door open.

Junior Dill rushed out and called, "What's going on?"

Brynne struggled to her feet and slumped against him, sobbing. Callie lunged at her.

Junior, his arm around Brynne, said, "Stop this!"

"This is what you get for screwing around with my boyfriend," Callie spat. She swung a punch. Brynne ducked and it landed on Junior's chest.

"Get out of here or I'll call the police," he told Callie.

She stepped back, scowling.

"Can I use your phone to call my mom to come and get me?" Brynne whimpered. "Mine's broke."

"You can call from the office," said Junior. He looked back at Callie. "Go on! Get out of here right now!"

As Callie slunk out of the gates and joined Stanton and Jessica, Junior asked Brynne, "I don't know you, do I? Are you at school here?"

Stanton thought, *Shit. He's suspicious.*

"Yeah. But I live out in...one of the villages," said Brynne. "Get bussed in every day. Hardly ever in town 'cept for school."

"And who's that you're fighting with?"

"She lives near me. All I did was smile at her stupid boyfriend while we were waiting for the bus yesterday and she thinks I like him. Then tonight my folks came to town to do some shopping so I came with them so I could hang around while they're at the store. My big treat, right? Next thing I know that skank comes out of nowhere and is all over me and I was scared and started running but she came after me and...."

Brynne collapsed against Junior, sobbing. Stanton marvelled at the ease with which the lies rolled out of her. Junior put his arm around her and patted her shoulder. "You'll be safe with me." He led her into the office.

Two minutes later they reappeared in the office doorway.

Brynne said, "Mom told me to wait by the gates."

Junior said, "Are you sure you'll be all right now?"

Brynne nodded and breathed, "Thank you. You've been so kind."

She set off for the gate, turning once to wave. Junior waved back, smiling, and returned to the office.

Brynne rejoined the others. "What an idiot."

"Well?" Callie asked.

Brynne spoke quickly and quietly. "Old-fashioned log drop construction. Three four-metre cradles. Two two-by-two concrete stanchions, crumbling in places. Two charges each. Easy."

"Timer?"

"No need. Thirty-second fuse will do it."

"Entry?"

"Over the fence behind the storage shed."

Stanton looked from one to the other. "What are you saying?"

"Just covering all the bases," said Callie.

Brynne said, "You planning on running to Daddy and telling him the nasty girls from EcoAction are plotting something?"

"'Course not."

"Good. 'Cause we got friends who'll make you sorry if you do. That's if Cal and me don't get to you first."

"Stanton's on our side," said Jessica, moving close to him and clutching his arm. "Like I said."

"And like Callie said—he better be," said Brynne.

SEVEN

The first person they saw back at the hall was Sergeant Munn.
He was standing just inside the door and he watched them
as they took their seats. Stanton's father had finished his talk
with a display of old photographs of the dam, laid out at the
front of the hall for the audience to file past and view. Verna
Mullen was talking.

"...and I'd like to thank Mr. Frame for his interesting and
illuminating account of the Black River Mill. Any questions?"

A short, round woman with grey hair stood and raised
her hand like a child in a classroom. She stared around as if
she'd forgotten what she was going to say. Stanton searched
for her name. He'd seen her kayaking on the lake. She lived
on the far shore opposite Mrs. Caithness.

Stanton's father prompted, "Go on, Mrs. Tuff."

She raised a shaking finger and pointed it at him. "I
blame the worry and the stress of the flood five years ago
for the heart attack that took my Joe. I spent everything he
left me getting the cabin repaired so I could stay in it, where
he'd lived all his life, and still feel like I had something of
him around me. TransNational gave me a thousand dollars,
which just about covered the cost of the dumpster that took
away pretty much everything we owned. I can't afford to fix
up the cabin if the lake floods again and I don't want to live
somewhere else. So if it's going to flood, I need to know,
Mr. Frame, so I can plan to go and join my Joe."

"I'm truly sorry, Mrs. Tuff," Stanton's father said quietly.

"I don't need your sympathy," she said. "I just need to know—will the lake flood again?"

"I'll do everything I can not to let it," Stanton's father said.

"You can start by opening the gates," Shingles yelled.

"Will you do that—open the gates?" Mrs. Tuff pressed.

"I can't right now," Stanton's father said. "But I won't let the river and the lake flood."

"Do you promise?" Mrs. Tuff asked.

Don't promise, Dad, Stanton thought. *You're setting yourself up. You can't control the river, or TransNational.*

"Yes," said his father. "I promise."

Mrs. Tuff murmured, "Thank you, Mr. Frame. That's all I need to hear."

The audience applauded as she sat. Stanton didn't know whether it was for Mrs. Tuff or his father.

Fred Shingles guffawed and shouted, "You may as well promise I'll become prime minister tomorrow."

"I'll vote for you, Fred," someone retorted. "You couldn't be any worse than the one we've got now."

As the audience laughed and applauded again, Stanton's father spoke quietly to the mayor.

"Would you like to come up here and make a presentation, Mr. Shingles?" she asked.

"Thought you'd never ask," Shingles said.

As he set off for the front of the hall, Sergeant Munn warned, "Keep a lid on it, Fred."

Shingles stood before the audience for a few seconds, his head down, his lips moving silently. A few people laughed.

"We're all waiting," one shouted.

"Saying your prayers, Fred?" jeered another.

Shingles raised his head and swept his eyes around the room. He seemed suddenly transformed into a statesman or a distinguished professor as he started.

"Records from the 1950s to the year 2006 show the average level of water in the Black River and Musquash Lake was thirteen metres between July and October, and fifteen metres between November and June."

He paced backwards and forwards as he spoke, his hands clasped behind his back, alternately looking at the ground as if gathering his thoughts, and surveying his audience.

"Only once in all that time did it rise above fifteen metres, in 1965, in the Great December Deluge some of you may remember, when the province received over fifteen centimetres of rain in twenty-four hours, and the river rose to almost seventeen metres. High—but not high enough for it or the lake to crest their banks. The only flood—not on record, but in folklore, according to the old-timers in the community—"

"Old-timers like you, Fred?" someone called.

No one laughed, and several people shushed the heckler.

Shingles ignored the jibe. "The only flood was over one hundred years ago, in the spring freshet. An ice jam, the sort Mr. Frame would dynamite these days, caused the river to overflow its banks near where the dam is now. Apart from that single aberration, water levels in the Black River and Musquash Lake have been models of consistency for as long as we have records."

He stopped pacing and paused before going on. "All that changed ten years ago when TransNational took over Black River Power. Since then, water levels have been at an all-time high, and the town has issued five flood warnings, one of which, as you know, preceded an actual flood, in which many of our houses suffered serious damage. The average water level is now seventeen metres. Critical level is eighteen metres."

He paused again and looked around at his silent audience. "I keep records, too, and my records show that for every centimetre of rain we receive, the river rises by a quarter of a metre with the dam open. If the dam is *closed*, that becomes three quarters of a metre. In the downpour of the last few days, we've received fifteen centimetres of rain, which means, with the dam closed, as Mr. Frame has acknowledged it is at this moment, the water will rise well above critical level. In other words—" Shingles broke off to make a show of looking at his watch before continuing. "In other words, in less than thirty hours from now, the river will flood."

There was instant uproar. People stood and pointed accusingly at Stanton's father. Some shook their fists.

"So why aren't the gates open?"

"What d'you say to that, Frame?"

Sergeant Munn moved to the side of the hall and gestured at the audience to calm down.

Fred Shingles waited for the commotion to subside before continuing. "TransNational Power is not just guilty of controlling water levels. It also controls the amount of rain we receive."

Stanton felt a beat in the room. It was like an aural double-take. He glanced at Jessica and murmured, "Did I hear that right?"

"Shit. I thought he was going to hold it together," she muttered.

Shingles, oblivious of the curious looks being passed among his audience, carried on. "The Canadian Record of Publicly Traded Companies shows TransNational has a controlling interest in several international airlines that fly jumbo jets, which makes sense when you think about it because of the millions of gallons of fuel they consume, much of it supplied, of course, by TransNational.

"Now, you've all seen the vapour trails these planes leave as they fly over Black River. You think nothing of them, but they are not just vapour trails. They contain a chemical agent that turns existing clouds into rain clouds. It's the same technology used in drought-stricken areas of the world to generate rain, and it's the reason, along with climate change, why our rainfall is so much greater and more intense than it used to be. And of course the more rain we get, the more water there is coming down the Black River, and the more power TransNational gets to generate, and the more money the company makes."

People were laughing quietly as they shook their heads and exchanged knowing looks. Sergeant Munn was moving towards the front of the room. Shingles, seeing him, spoke louder and faster.

"TransNational also adds chemicals to the Black River as it passes through their turbines so every time you turn something on in your house the chemicals are released and you breathe them in and they get in your brain and dull the frontal lobes that give you the ability to reason and criticize. In other words, TransNational stops you saying or doing anything to oppose it, so it can do whatever it likes."

Someone shouted, "So how come it doesn't affect you, Fred?"

Shingles smiled slyly. "'Cause there's no power coming into my house."

As the laughter grew, Shingles ranted, "TransNational controls the river and the weather and your brains, but we can stop them by getting rid of the dam. If you won't help, I'll do it myself. You think I'm joking and I'm crazy but I'm trained in sabotage and I've got explosives ready to go, so let's see who's laughing when the dam gets blown sky high."

Shingles's voice was lost in the riot of laughter and jeers and whistles and applause.

"You tell 'em, Fred," someone called.

Sergeant Munn was moving in on Shingles. Jessica jumped up and hurried down the other side of the hall. Stanton, after a moment's hesitation, followed her. She reached Shingles first.

She took his arm, stilling his pacing, and murmured, "Hey, Fred. Why don't you sit with me? I saved a seat for you."

Sergeant Munn said, "Good move, Jess. Thanks," and retreated.

As Jessica and Stanton led Shingles to a seat at the back of the room, they passed Callie and Brynne heading the other way. They stood at the front of the hall, Callie surveying the crowd, Brynne, hands in pockets, looking at her feet.

When the commotion that had followed Shingles's tirade died down, and the audience's attention started to settle on the newcomers, Callie asked Verna Mullen, "May I speak?"

The mayor nodded, and Callie started. "I'm Callie and this is Brynne. We're from BC—"

One of the mill workers sitting near Stanton muttered, "So why don't you go back there?"

"—and we belong to an environmental organization called EcoAction."

"Tree huggers," the mill worker said, louder. Two more mill workers sitting in front of Stanton turned around and nodded in agreement. At the front, Charlie Hatt looked at Adam Glennie and rolled his eyes.

"We're monitoring TransNational Power's hydroelectric projects in at least a dozen countries around the world, as well as here in Canada," Callie went on.

"Why?" someone called out. "I thought hydroelectric power was supposed to be good for the environment."

"Usually it is," said Callie. "But TransNational wants to generate maximum power from each development, and in order to do that, it has to enlarge the headpond, which means destroying lowlands that are not only fertile and productive, but also sustain plant and animal life. By manipulating the water level in the Black River and Musquash Lake so what's considered normal has gradually risen—as Mr. Shingles pointed out—TransNational is kind of enlarging the headpond by stealth."

The audience was listening to Callie but looking at Brynne, who slouched with her hands in her pockets, one long, bare leg planted slightly in front of the other, one hip thrust sideways, like a model.

Sergeant Munn was making notes.

Callie looked around again before asking, "Who lives near the river or on the lakeshore?"

"What's it got to do with you where anyone lives?" someone called out.

"Give the girl a chance," another countered.

Two dozen people raised their hands.

"Well, look out," said Callie. "TransNational has plans to increase its ability to generate power, and your homes will be the first to go."

Stanton's father, who had been listening carefully, started up. "Wait. That's not true. I know nothing about it."

Stanton remembered TransNational's secret plan to modernize the dam. Did that include increasing power generation?

"I believe you, sir," said Callie. "No one knows about it except the very highest executives, and they certainly wouldn't bother to inform a small subsidiary like Black River Power."

"So how come you know?" Stanton's father asked.

"We have informers," said Callie.

There was a beat of silence again, this time not of surprise, but of apprehension.

Stanton thought, *What kind of organization has informers?* It made EcoAction sound menacing and sinister and strangely powerful. And who were the informers? Were they politicians or in the upper ranks of TransNational itself?

"Why are you here?" a woman asked quietly.

"To help you," said Callie. "Because TransNational does not have a good record of treating the environment responsibly or of dealing fairly with people affected by its projects."

"How can you help?" the woman asked.

"By stopping construction, at least temporarily, like we have at the Little Beaver Falls hydro project in Montana, and the Grand Falls Gorge project in Nova Scotia, and the La Yesca hydroelectric project in Mexico."

"And just how d'you think you're going to manage that?" Todd Hanley scoffed.

"By taking TransNational to court," said Callie. "And with demonstrations and stuff like that."

Stanton thought of what he'd read online: bomb threats and explosions linked to EcoAction, the bus hijacked and burnt, rocks and Molotov cocktails thrown at police. Was that what Callie meant by "stuff like that"?

She was still talking. "The construction of dams has already caused the forced relocation of over fifty million people all over the world, and—"

Verna Mullen interrupted. "We're here to talk about Black River, not world affairs."

"Sorry," said Callie. "Let me finish by asking a question. Who owns the Black River?"

"What do you mean?" Verna Mullen asked.

"Does Mr. Frame own it?"

"Of course not," said Stanton's father.

"Does Black River Power own it?"

"No!" Fred Shingles shouted.

"Does TransNational Power own it?" Callie asked, her voice growing louder with each question.

Several people in the audience responded, as well as Shingles. "No!"

"Does the government own it?"

Brynne, suddenly changing her stance for the first time, thrust a pointing finger at the crowd, cueing the response.

"No!" came from the audience.

"Does the Town of Black River own it?"

"No!" Most people in the hall were shouting the answer now.

Brynne pumped her fist in the air with each shouted "No!" She looked like a revolutionary. Stanton pictured her wrapped in a flag, a rifle in one hand, the other raised in a salute with fist clenched. Jessica jumped to her feet. People around her followed suit.

Stanton, about to stand, saw his father watching him. He hesitated. If he stood, siding with EcoAction against the company, would it be a total betrayal of his father?

But he'd often enough heard him rail against the company, and seen his frustration at having to do as the company dictated although he knew it was wrong. And now there was a plan to increase the generation of power, which it seemed the company had not even told his father about. Stanton believed his father would stand, too, if he didn't work for TransNational. If Stanton stood, he told himself, it would be as much for his father as for himself. He'd do it on his behalf.

And he'd do it not for EcoAction—he could not care less about them—but for Jessica, because he admired her concern and her passion for the environment, and agreed with her about the damage TransNational was doing to it. He also did it to please her and out of love for her, although they never spoke of love. They didn't need to. What did love mean, anyway? They hung out, they spent time together as much as they could, they enjoyed one another's company, they liked the same things, they were friends, they made out, and they never argued, at least until the ride from the lake to town. If that wasn't love, what was?

His father smiled, shrugged, nodded. It was like permission to betray.

Stanton stood with Jessica.

"Do the people who live on its banks own it?" Callie shouted.

Another fist pump from Brynne.

The response was a roar. "No!"

"So—who owns the river?" Callie pressed.

"All of us," Fred Shingles thundered. "We own the river!"

Callie echoed the rhythm of Shingles's declaration. "Who owns the river?"

The audience, catching on immediately, responded, "We own the river!" More people stood and repeated, "We own the river!" Someone clapped with the beat of the words. Others joined in and within seconds most of the people in the hall were chanting and clapping and stamping and repeating, "We own the river!"

Amid the chanting Stanton heard shouts of "Tell that to your bosses, Mr. Frame," and "Screw TransNational!"

Jessica grabbed and hugged Stanton while she continued the chant. Her eyes shone. Still chanting, she released him and skipped to the front of the hall, where she stood beside Brynne, pumping her fist in unison with her as the crowd chanted.

Stanton followed Jessica but stood at the side, his eyes roving between her, his father, and the crowd.

Sergeant Munn was watching Callie and Brynne as he talked urgently on his cell.

Stanton's mother had joined Fred Shingles at the back of the hall and they were talking, their heads close.

Stanton's father and Les Cuff were staring at one another. Stanton's father gestured hopelessly. Les shrugged.

Verna Mullen said weakly, "I declare the meeting closed."

It was nine o'clock. Just over twenty-four hours to flood time.

People started filing from the hall, some still chanting. Jessica was huddled with Callie and Brynne.

Stanton asked, "Ready to go?"

"See if Fred needs a ride to the lake," Jessica suggested.

Stanton made his way to the back of the hall, where his mother and Shingles were still talking. As Stanton approached, he heard his mother say, "That's good, Fred. We'll talk about it later."

EIGHT

The first call came just after 6:00 A.M. on the hotel line. It woke Stanton in the room adjoining his parents'. He heard his father speaking. At the same time as his father ended the call his cell rang. He had another brief conversation. There was a knock at Stanton's door and his father said, "Are you awake?"

Stanton grunted.

His father opened the door. "Sorry about the phone."

"Not your fault. What's up?"

"Old Mrs. Cline on Riverside wanted to know where she should go when the river floods."

"What'd you tell her?"

"Red Cross is setting up an emergency shelter at the community hall. Verna Mullen told me last night but didn't want to announce it at the meeting because she was afraid people would worry even more than they are already. Then Dave Watson called. He's on patrol upriver. Says the water's over the bank all the way from Black River to Big Pond and only a few metres from a dozen homes."

Stanton's mother put her head around the door and said, "Let's have breakfast and get away from at least one phone for a while." The room phone rang again. Stanton's father went to answer it but she ordered, "Leave it," then took his arm and led him from the room.

Friday was usually a popular day for business meetings over breakfast at the motel but Stanton and his parents were the only people in the restaurant. While his father moved away to take another call on his cell, his mother whispered, "I told him to tell the desk not to put any calls through and to shut his cell off, but he says he has to be available to answer people's concerns about the river. He's hardly slept, worrying about it flooding."

His father returned to the table. His cell rang. He started to rise but Stanton's mother put her hand on his arm and said, "You'd better eat as you talk or you'll never eat at all."

He muttered, "Excuse me," and took the call at the table. Stanton heard Junior's voice. "The phone won't stop ringing."

"Same here. It's because you got what you wanted. The dam's closed and there'll be a flood sometime tonight, sixteen or seventeen hours from now, so people are freaking out."

"Can I get someone in to answer it?"

"No."

"So what am I supposed to tell them?"

"Same as me. Tell them to get ready for a flood."

"Company won't like us saying that."

"You think I care?"

Stanton's father ended the call.

A man, unshaven and with bloodshot eyes and hair awry, burst into the restaurant. He marched to where Stanton's father sat and stood over him as he snarled, "I guessed you'd be in here having a nice breakfast while your dam floods the town again."

Stanton searched for his name.

"If you'd like to sit down we can discuss your concerns, Mr. Cleghorn," his father said.

Miller Cleghorn. He lived alone in a shack close to the river on the road out of town. A lean, snarling dog, something between a whippet and a German shepherd, flung itself to the end of its chain every time Stanton walked past.

"I don't have time to sit around like you," Cleghorn growled. "I've got stuff to move out, stove and furniture and freezer and all, and I don't know where I'm going to put everything, and I've been up the last two nights watching the river, half the town with me, and all you do is sit here having breakfast. I've a good mind to…."

His voice was getting louder, threatening, and his fist was raised and clenched. Stanton sized him up. They were about the same height, but Cleghorn was bulkier, broader across the shoulders. Stanton set himself to take him down if he moved to deliver on his threat. One arm around his neck and a kick in the back of the knees should do it, like he'd learned from play fighting with his father.

Stanton wished his father would match Cleghorn's belligerence. Was he so stricken with guilt at his forced siding with TransNational that he wouldn't defend himself?

A voice cut across the restaurant. "Mr. Cleghorn, you will leave the restaurant now."

Cleghorn looked around. Looked back at Stanton's father.

Sergeant Munn stood in the restaurant doorway and said, "*Now*, Mr. Cleghorn."

Miller Cleghorn glared at Stanton's father for a few seconds before stalking from the room.

Sergeant Munn ambled across to where they sat. "Want me to charge him with threat and assault?"

Stanton's father shook his head. "He's just frustrated and worried."

"Still, you don't have to put up with that kind of foolishness." Sergeant Munn sat heavily and yawned. "Sorry to disturb your breakfast, folks. I guessed you'd all be up."

Stanton's mother poured him coffee. "Late night, Ernie?"

"It was by the time I'd written my reports and finished up at the office."

"Anything to deal with after the meeting?" Stanton's father asked.

Sergeant Munn grinned. "You mean after Miss Jost and Miss Tanner whipped the crowd into a frenzy? Nothing much. A bit of shouting. What was it? 'The river belongs to us.' A few people hanging around on Main, mostly just talking. There wasn't mayhem in the streets of Black River, if that's what you're thinking, despite the efforts of Jessica and Stanton's new friends." He winked at Stanton.

"Not friends," said Stanton. "I'd never met them before last night."

He was instantly ashamed. Why was he distancing himself from Callie and Brynne, when last night he'd admired Callie's eloquence, and how she and Brynne had stirred the crowd, and what a striking figure Brynne had cut? He tried to come up with something in their defence, but Sergeant Munn was still talking.

"You got back to the hotel okay."

Stanton's father nodded. "Did you think I'd need police protection?"

"You got it, anyway. I had Dave Watson keep a discreet eye on you, and cruise around the hotel a few times in the night."

"Thanks. But not necessary, surely."

Sergeant Munn shrugged. "Best to be safe. Word is EcoAction is sending more of its followers to Black River. They may be here already. Their actions can be…unpredictable." He turned to Stanton. "What do you know about EcoAction?"

"Not much. Just what I found on the web. They want to protect the environment."

"That's a good thing," said Sergeant Munn. "It's how they go about it sometimes that bothers me—and others. You and Jess best be careful."

Stanton's father was staring at Stanton. He said, "So they're—what—some kind of extremists? Why didn't you tell me about them before the meeting? I might have been better prepared for what happened."

Stanton shrugged. "I only found out about them just before the meeting. Didn't have time to tell you." He wondered if he would have even if he'd had time. And if he'd warned his father, would that have constituted betrayal of Callie and Brynne (and by extension, Jessica)? Would it have been enough for them to carry out their threat of reprisal? He went on. "Anyway, Callie and Brynne seem... nice. They don't exactly look like terrorists, do they?"

"What does a terrorist look like?" Sergeant Munn asked. He sighed. "Don't get me wrong. I'm sure they're fine young ladies and I admire their passion for what they believe in. But it's my job to be cautious, and I don't want to see you and Jess getting mixed up with something that gets out of hand. That's all."

"That goes for me, too," said Stanton's father.

Sergeant Munn stood up. "Thanks for the coffee. Willis, I need a quiet word—if you'll excuse us, please, Angie, Stanton."

He took Stanton's father aside and they spoke in low voices. Stanton caught "EcoAction" and "trouble" before they moved out of earshot.

Stanton muttered, "They're not terrorists. Mr. Shingles is more of a terrorist than them."

His mother smiled. "Fred's no terrorist either."

Stanton suddenly remembered his mother's conversation with Mrs. Caithness's neighbour as the meeting broke up.

"Mom, what were you talking about with Mr. Shingles after the meeting last night? You both looked totally serious. And I heard you say you'd talk to him again."

Stanton's mother laughed. "Poor Fred. I wanted to make sure he wasn't about to do something stupid with all that fire power he's got stashed at his cabin."

"You know about the guns and the explosives?"

"Of course I do. Sergeant Munn knows, too, and he keeps your father informed, with Fred being so set against the mill to the point of threatening it, as you heard last night. But I'm sure it's just talk. Fred was always a great talker. It's what he did best when he was teaching."

"Mr. Shingles was a teacher?"

"He taught me in high school. It's a part of his life he'd prefer to forget, and have others forget. He was let go for 'subversive activity.'"

"Cool. What kind of subversive activity?"

"He taught social sciences and he was accused of bringing politics into the classroom."

"Did he?"

"You bet. He was always criticizing the government—and the opposition. We loved him for it, but the administration wasn't so keen. The superintendent told him he could resign or have a charge of unprofessional conduct brought against him. He told the superintendent he could shove the charge and the job up…well, you know where." She sighed and poured herself another cup of coffee. "He was in his fifties then but still quite a dashing figure with his long white hair and his looks—he was kind of craggy in those days—and his passion for his subject. He was friends with your grandfather and often came to the house. It wasn't until I went away that I lost touch with him."

"Yesterday, when I saw him at the lake, he said he worked for Black River Power."

"Only for about a year after his teaching career. Your dad had to let him go, he was so unreliable."

Sergeant Munn left and Stanton's father returned to the table.

"Emergency Measures has ordered the evacuation of all homes likely to be flooded. The police and fire department are carrying out the evacuations. They're setting up an evacuation centre at the community hall. TransNational is sending people to help. They're already on the way from Port Carleton. Sergeant Munn gave me a list of all the people to be evacuated." He looked at Stanton. "Jessica and her grandmother are on the list."

NINE

After breakfast, Stanton set out to walk to the lake. It was still only 8:00 A.M. The countdown clock running in his head told him the river would flood at midnight.

He wanted badly to see Jessica. After the meeting, he'd driven her, with Callie and Brynne, to the boat launch. They'd talked excitedly all the way about the meeting, and how Callie and Brynne had won over the crowd and set them chanting. The two had sat in the back seat and Jessica's head had been turned towards them all the way. At the lake she'd leaned towards Stanton to kiss him goodnight but he'd leaned away. Two could play at the distance game. She'd shrugged and climbed from the car. He didn't bother to get out and the last he'd seen of them was the lights on the boat as it headed towards the point. The last he'd heard, the throaty chug of the boat's ten-horsepower outboard motor.

As he rounded the last bend in the road to the lake he saw a car parked near the top of the boat ramp, which was now almost completely under water. A man sat at the wheel. Stanton approached the car on foot, wondering whether the driver needed directions.

An open boat with two powerful outboard engines sped around the point, coming from the direction of Mrs. Caithness's cabin, and headed for shore. At the last moment it slowed, sending a wave washing beyond the ramp and up the road past the car so that Stanton had to jump backwards to keep his feet dry.

Three men were in the boat, one of them Fred Shingles, who sat with a bowed head and a blanket around his shoulders. The driver jumped from the car and ran to meet it. While the man at the tiller idled the motor and steadied the boat at the ramp, his companion pulled Shingles up and pushed him towards where the driver was now holding the bow. Shingles climbed out and the driver took his arm. Shingles's pants and shoes were wet. He shuffled towards the car, his head down, the driver still holding his arm.

"You okay, Mr. Shingles?" Stanton called.

Shingles looked up. He didn't seem to recognize Stanton.

"Keep clear, please," the driver warned.

"Where are you taking him?" Stanton asked.

"Evacuation centre."

"I don't think Mr. Shingles wants to be evacuated." Stanton moved towards Shingles. "Do you, Mr. Shingles?"

The driver put his arm up to stop Stanton. "He doesn't have a choice. And I told you to keep clear."

He bundled Shingles into the car and drove off. The boat backed away from the ramp and swung towards the point, its prow riding high as it took off fast.

Stanton called Jessica.

Before he could speak she said, "Two men took Fred away. He didn't want to go."

"I know. I just saw them. I'm at the boat launch. They're heading back your way, evacuating people. They must be from TransNational. I'd know them if they were police or fire department."

"Grandma doesn't want to go. Neither do I."

"Can you take off in the boat? Hide out in the cove up the shore, maybe?"

"Callie and Brynne are out in it, getting evidence of environmental damage to use in a court case against TransNational."

"I'll be there as quick as I can."

Stanton set off at a run on the woods road. He'd gone less than thirty metres when he encountered ankle-deep water flowing from the lake and across the road. He took off his shoes and socks, tied the laces, and hung them in a tree. Then he rolled up his pant legs, hoping he could wade to the higher ground where the cabin stood, and set off again. He gasped as he stepped into the water and its chill shot from his feet to his head. He kept going but within a few more metres, the water was above his knees and getting deeper.

Stanton splashed back to where he'd left his shoes and socks. He pulled off his toque and stripped off his pants and shirt. As he stepped out of his pants, his cell phone fell from his pocket. Realizing he'd probably need it, he wracked his brain for a way to keep it dry. He felt in all his pockets but found nothing of use. He looked all around on the ground and in the underbrush at each side of the trail. Nothing. His eye fell on his toque, lying on the ground where he'd thrown it with his shirt and pants. Maybe if he crammed the toque tightly on his head with the cell phone inside, he could get it safely to the cabin. He'd have to keep his head above water, but it was so cold he planned to do that anyway. He balanced the phone on his head and pulled the toque tightly over it. Stanton shook his head. The phone hardly moved. *The worst that can happen is I need a new phone*, he thought.

He gathered his clothes and hung them in the tree with his shoes and socks. He removed his glasses, tucked them down the front of his underwear, and ran into the flood. As soon as the water was up to his waist, he made a graceless running dive and started swimming up the road.

Instantly the current carried him away from the lake. He corrected his course but swimming against the flow and the cold temperature slowed his progress. He had to struggle to keep his head above water.

A young birch tree, its muddy roots sticking up like a fan, shot past in front of him. Something bumped against his legs. He glanced back and saw chunks of firewood bobbing in the current. Half a dozen beer bottles and a red basketball bobbed with them. A cat, eyes wide in terror, was swept past. Stanton reached to grab it but missed and it disappeared across the road. Neither Mrs. Caithness nor Fred Shingles had a cat and he wondered where it had come from. Clumps of grass scoured from the lakeside dragged past in the muddy, roiling torrent, unrecognizable from the placid, benign water where he and Jessica swam and kayaked in the summer.

His arms were tired and as he moved slower the current threatened to carry him across the road and away from the bluff. He wondered where he'd fetch up if he was carried away like the cat. Either he'd end up on the higher ground alongside the lake road he'd just driven on, or he'd be swept around it as the lake water sought lower ground and joined the river, which it surely would if it hadn't already. Then he'd be carried downriver to the dam, which at least was closed so he had a chance of not hurtling over the falls but instead risked getting carried into the turbines. Was that the cat's fate? Or would it find something to cling to on the way and haul itself out?

He was alongside the bluff. He could see the gap in the trees where the trail wound up to the cabin. He had to turn and swim directly against the current but he wasn't making any progress; he could barely hold himself against it.

Something brushed his legs. He felt under the water. Spindly, wiry branches. The alders that grew beside the woods road before they gave way to the cedars on this side of the bluff. He grabbed a handful of stems and pulled himself hand over hand from one alder bush to the next until he reached calmer water in the lee of the bluff.

His feet touched land and he plunged forward through the alders, which tore at his feet and legs until he crawled out of the flood and onto the trail. He looked down at his legs, red and raw from the cold, and streaked with mud and blood. At least he still had his underwear and glasses and cell. He pulled off his toque. The phone was dry. He tucked it in his underwear, swapping it for his glasses, and ran up the trail to Jessica's grandmother's cabin.

The evacuation boat was pulled up to the bluff and tied to a young birch tree. The rope was taut and the birch was bent as the current sucked at the boat.

One man held Jessica in a bear hug by the cabin door while the other carried her grandmother in a fireman's lift over the rocks towards the boat. They were the same men Stanton had encountered at the boat ramp. Jessica was wriggling and kicking backwards at the man's ankles and Mrs. Caithness was flailing her fists at her abductor's back. Stanton ran past them and untied the boat. It rocked and bucked, straining against his grip.

"Hey!" he shouted. "Let them go and get off their land or I'll strand you here and you'll lose your boat."

"You've been told once to keep out of this," the man holding Jessica warned.

Stanton didn't answer, he just paid the rope out as far as it would go until he held only the end. The boat lurched and swung wildly in the current.

"We're acting on behalf of the police and EMO," the man with Mrs. Caithness said.

"Like I care," Stanton said. "You got five seconds to get the hell out of here. One, two…."

The man slowly set Mrs. Caithness down.

She held her finger centimetres from his nose and spat, "If my husband was alive he'd have kicked the crap out of you the moment you set foot on the bluff."

Jessica's captor released her and jumped away as she aimed a kick at his shins. Stanton pulled the boat in and the men climbed aboard.

The man at the tiller snarled, "You'll be hearing from the police about this."

Stanton threw the rope in the boat and they took off across the lake.

Mrs. Caithness patted Stanton's shoulder. "Our gallant knight. Thank you."

Jessica ran to him and threw herself against him. She was crying and breathing heavily. Stanton could feel her shaking. He held her with both arms and she pushed herself into him.

He felt her begin to relax and she murmured, "I like your outfit."

"Enough of that, you two. Let's have some tea and get you warm, Stanton," Mrs. Caithness said.

In the cabin Jessica wrapped a blanket around him and sat close. The power was out but the wood stove was going and it was warm. Mrs. Caithness filled the kettle from the cabin's spring-fed water supply and made tea.

Jessica said, "Grandma wants a couple of baskets of wood in the loft. Then as long as we only get a few centimetres of water in the cabin we can keep the stove going and it'll be warm up there."

"You fill the basket and I'll haul it up," said Stanton.

He climbed the ladder to the loft and Jessica went outside to the woodpile. While he waited for the first basket he looked around at the clutter of Mrs. Caithness's furniture and possessions and the sleeping quarters squeezed in among them. Jessica's cot and her grandmother's bed nest were surrounded by piles of clothes. Callie and Brynne's sleeping bags lay among stacks of books piled on chairs. A few pages stapled together into a crude manual lay between the sleeping bags. The title on the front page read *EcoAction. Dynamite 101: How to Blow Up Anything.* Stanton opened it and started to read.

Jessica called from below, "Ready?"

He lay over the edge of the loft, reached down, and hauled the basket up. He emptied it and passed it back down. While Jessica refilled it he photographed the manual with his cell phone.

After they'd brought in the second basket of logs, Mrs. Caithness poured tea.

Jessica said, "This time tomorrow the water will be running through here unless your dad can persuade the company to let him open the dam."

"No way is TransNational going to back down," said Stanton.

"So someone else will have to open it—and make sure it stays open," said Jessica.

Stanton stared at her. "Like—who? And how?"

Jessica shrugged and looked out across the lake, avoiding his eye. Stanton felt a catch of fear in his throat.

TEN

When Callie and Brynne returned, Jessica suggested they all take the boat and go to town for groceries because if the flood lasted more than a few days there'd be a run on food. They tied the boat near the ramp and after Stanton had retrieved his clothes from the tree on the woods road they walked to town.

Before they hit the SaveEasy they stopped at Black River Java. Tess greeted Stanton: "I thought your dad was going to open the dam."

"He thought so too," said Stanton. "But the company overruled him."

He knew his father didn't like him divulging company business but thought the greater betrayal would be not to let it be known that the closing of the dam was against his wishes.

Tess went on. "Did you hear about Fred Shingles?"

"Just that he got evacuated."

"He went on a rant at the evacuation centre—you know how he gets—and they couldn't get him to calm down so they called the police and Dave Watson came and he took a swing at him. Dave arrested him for assaulting a police officer."

Two men Stanton recognized from the mill came in and while Tess served them, Stanton took his coffee and joined Jessica, Callie, and Brynne at a table by the window. The mill workers took a table nearby.

Sergeant Munn drove slowly past.

One of the mill workers said loudly, "Strangers who got no business here should go back where they came from and stop stirring up trouble, meddling in stuff that's got nothing to do with them."

Stanton muttered, "Ignore him." He hoped it didn't sound too much like a plea.

Callie sat with her back to the men. Without moving she said, "You talking about us?"

"If the shoe fits," said the man.

"We'll go when we're ready," said Callie.

"When'll that be?" the man's companion asked.

"When the job's done," said Callie, still not moving.

"What job's that?" said the first man.

Callie turned and looked at the mill workers. "Stopping TransNational from wrecking the environment and people's lives."

Sergeant Munn drove past again, heading in the other direction. He parked in sight of the coffee shop.

"You come here and set folks one against the other, family members and friends, all because you got some bee in your bonnet about the environment from watching too much TV and because you've never had a real job in your life," said the first man.

His companion picked up the thread. "Then you and your dyke friend will move on and do the same thing some-place else and upset another community while we're left to pick up the pieces here."

Brynne laughed. "Tough shit, turd brain."

"What did you call me?" the man said.

He stood and took a step towards her. His companion stood, too. Stanton, sitting beside Brynne, saw something in her hands, which lay demurely in her lap.

"You heard," said Callie.

She nodded to Brynne, who slipped something on her right hand. Knuckle dusters. He'd never seen them before and had thought they existed only in old gangster movies.

Brynne stood. Jessica looked from Brynne to the mill workers. Tess watched nervously from behind the counter.

"Take it back, bitch," the mill worker threatened. He raised a hand, pointing at Brynne.

Stanton had visions of an all-out rumble in Black River Java, Brynne lacerating the faces of his father's colleagues.

He stood and said, "Let's all calm down, guys."

From the corner of his eye he saw Sergeant Munn, still in his car, staring at him as he talked on his radio.

"Keep out of this, Frame," one of the men said.

It was the second time that morning Stanton had been told to keep out of something. He couldn't remember ever having been told it before. He felt almost proud.

One of the mill workers noticed the shiny studs on Brynne's hand. "Jesus, girl. Just who are you?"

Callie, still sitting, answered for her. "A friend of the people TransNational is trampling over."

Brynne's stance was that of the night before, slouching, one long leg slightly in front of the other, one hip thrust sideways, a picture of fuck-you cool. Not just a revolutionary, but a revolutionary warrior ready to take on an army. She cocked her head, half smiling, and said quietly, "Well, boys, what you gonna do?"

The door opened and Les Cuff came in. He looked from the mill workers to Stanton's table. "What's going on, guys?"

One of the mill workers muttered, "Nothing." He and his companion sat down.

Brynne snorted and led Callie and Jessica out.

Stanton, following, caught Cuff's eye.

Cuff murmured, "All right?"

"Thanks."

Outside on the sidewalk Stanton said lightly, "Seems like people are getting a little tense."

"Yeah. Maybe time to bring in the troops and step up the action," said Brynne.

Callie looked at her sharply and gave a quick shake of her head. Stanton just caught it. He had the feeling of being excluded again. He wondered if Jessica knew what Brynne meant, what Callie didn't want him to know. He remembered Jessica's comment the night before about someone outside the company opening the dam and making sure it stayed open.

As they split up—Stanton to go to the hotel to shower and change, the others to get groceries—he whispered to Jessica, "What did Brynne mean, bring in the troops and step up the action?"

Jessica glanced towards Callie and Brynne, who were already sauntering along Main Street. "Dunno. They don't tell me everything EcoAction's up to."

"Because of me, right? They think you'll tell me and I'll blab to Dad."

She shrugged, hugged him quickly, and hurried after Callie and Brynne.

Stanton didn't know whether to believe her. Maybe she knew what "bring in the troops and step up the action" meant but she wasn't going to say because she didn't trust him any more than Callie and Brynne did. Again he felt her drifting away from him, caught in a current of extremism and self-righteous moral absolutism he couldn't share.

He turned away to walk to the hotel and found Sergeant Munn on the sidewalk beside his car. He said, "I hear you had a little set-to with some of the rescuers from

TransNational." He grinned. "Good on you, looking after the ladies. The rescuers overstepped their mark, treating Mrs. Caithness and Jess like that. I told 'em so."

"I saw them bring Mr. Shingles off the lake. They set him off. It wasn't his fault: he was upset."

"Don't worry about Fred. If he'd limited himself to hitting out at one of the rescue guys we could have overlooked it. But taking a swing at Constable Dave? We couldn't let that go, although we won't pursue it."

ELEVEN

Stanton set off for the hotel. The town felt shot through with tension and anticipation. Friday was delivery day at the stores and usually the beeping of tractor trailers reversing into unloading bays at the SaveEasy and the Food Mart echoed around the centre of town. Today there was silence. Friday was Seniors' Fellowship Morning at the Baptist church but a notice on the door said *Fellowship cancelled today.* Carmichael's Country Diner, usually packed on a Friday morning, was empty except for a solitary man who sat in the window and gave Stanton the finger as he walked past. Stanton knew it was because he was Willis Frame's son, and that put him in TransNational's camp, responsible for the coming flood.

He strolled on.

As he passed the hardware store he glanced in the window. Farquarson's Original Drain Cleaner was on display at a special price. Drain cleaner was the first item on the list of ingredients in the EcoAction manual.

He pulled out his cell phone. The time on the screen leapt out at him: 10:30 A.M. Thirteen and a half hours until the river flooded. He scrolled through the pages he'd photographed and read the list of ingredients. He scrolled down to the How To section:"The size, construction, age, and condition of your target will determine the strength of the blast and the number of charges you will have to lay."

Brynne had talked after her reconnaissance about the two stanchions of the dam each needing two charges. Stanton knew better. There was a place on one of the stanchions a couple of metres from the top where the concrete was crumbling and there was a hole you could get your fist in and pull out chunks of masonry—or place explosives. His father often grumbled about it, and about TransNational's slowness in going ahead with the new dam, saying there'd be a time soon when the stanchion would be unsafe, and if it went, the whole dam would go with it.

One charge would do it.

As Brynne said—easy.

Easier than she thought.

With his cell phone open at the page of ingredients Stanton went in and picked up a basket. Mrs. Whittier at the check-out smiled at him. She wasn't that old—not much more than fifty, he thought—but since a fall from her bicycle two years before she'd worn a perpetual frown of anxiety and worry. She was constantly trying to put the fragments of her memory in order; while she could stack shelves and manage the cash, she searched for names all the time, even the people she saw every day, and sometimes forgot her address and telephone number. He saw her rummaging through her memory, searching for his name. Usually he supplied it, but not today.

"Good morning, er, Brian."

Good.

"Morning, Mrs. Whittier."

He set off through the rows of shelves, looking for the plumbing section. He found six varieties of drain cleaner. Which would be best? He compared the contents of each. They seemed pretty much the same. He supposed any one would do for making a bomb. He looked at the next two ingredients listed. Searched through the aisles and found several varieties of each.

Was it really this easy?

He fell into a daydream as he roamed the aisles, basket in one hand and cell in the other. He pictured Jessica scoffing at his assertion that he might resort to direct action if every other way of protesting had failed and there was nothing else to try. He cringed at the memory of Callie and Brynne's dismissal of him. He wanted to prove himself to Jessica; didn't want her to feel he'd let her down, didn't want her to be afraid to trust him. He imagined her admiration if he proved he was capable of direct action, and Callie and Brynne's acceptance and trust and approval, and his father's shock but secret pride because Stanton had done what Willis Frame dreamed of doing himself.

And it would be so easy to get out on the dam for the few seconds it would take. He knew exactly the spot to make for and when a good time would be. If anyone challenged him all he had to say was he was looking for his father.

He took another turn through the shelves, calculating. For a little over one hundred dollars he could cause mayhem. The store was quiet, no one around to remember his being there. Mrs. Whittier was still the only one on the cash. Even if she remembered seeing him in the store, she certainly wouldn't remember his name or what he'd bought.

He set off through the aisles again.

TWELVE

Stanton looked from his father to his mother. His arrival had obviously stopped their conversation. He said, "Sorry. I'll see if Mr. Cuff and the others need help."

He'd showered and changed and wanted to check in with his parents at the mill before rejoining Jessica. Les Cuff and Todd Hanley were greasing the winches out on the dam. Junior Dill was with them. He and Stanton had arrived at the mill at the same time. Stanton had commented, "You're in early," and Junior said, "Thought I'd check how things are. See if your dad needs help."

Stanton started backing out of the office.

His father said, "We're not talking secrets. It's just your mom's worried about your Aunt Jodie…."

"That's not what we were talking about, Willis, and you know it," said Stanton's mother. "All I said was Jodie doesn't seem to be getting over this latest flare-up and I was wondering if I should go and see her and I could tell you weren't really listening so I said what's on your mind and you told me and that's what we were talking about."

"Told you what?" Stanton asked.

His mother looked at his father. "Are you going to tell Stanton or shall I?"

"Go ahead," said Stanton's father. "You're going to anyway."

"He's going to quit," she said.

Stanton stared at his father, who protested, "I didn't say that. I said I was thinking about it."

n his father to his mother. *His arrival had*
their conversation. He said, "Sorry. I'll see
e others need help."

and changed and wanted to check in with
nill before rejoining Jessica. Les Cuff and
e greasing the winches out on the dam.
ith them. He and Stanton had arrived at
e time. Stanton had commented, "You're
ior said, "Thought I'd check how things
d needs help."

backing out of the office.

, "We're not talking secrets. It's just your
out your Aunt Jodie...."

at we were talking about, Willis, and you
ton's mother. "All I said was Jodie doesn't
g over this latest flare-up and I was won—
go and see her and I could tell you weren't
I said what's on your mind and you told
t we were talking about."

t?" Stanton asked.

oked at his father. "Are you going to tell
?"

d Stanton's father. "You're going to anyway."
quit," she said.

at his father, who protested, "I didn't say
hinking about it."

ELEVEN

Stanton set off for the hotel. The town felt shot through with
tension and anticipation. Friday was delivery day at the
stores and usually the beeping of tractor trailers reversing
into unloading bays at the SaveEasy and the Food Mart
echoed around the centre of town. Today there was silence.
Friday was Seniors' Fellowship Morning at the Baptist
church but a notice on the door said *Fellowship cancelled to-*
day. Carmichael's Country Diner, usually packed on a Friday morning, was empty except for a solitary man who sat
in the window and gave Stanton the finger as he walked
past. Stanton knew it was because he was Willis Frame's son,
and that put him in TransNational's camp, responsible for
the coming flood.

He strolled on.

As he passed the hardware store he glanced in the window. Farquarson's Original Drain Cleaner was on display
at a special price. Drain cleaner was the first item on the list
of ingredients in the EcoAction manual.

He pulled out his cell phone. The time on the screen
leapt out at him: 10:30 A.M. Thirteen and a half hours until the river flooded. He scrolled through the pages he'd
photographed and read the list of ingredients. He scrolled
down to the How To section: "The size, construction, age,
and condition of your target will determine the strength of
the blast and the number of charges you will have to lay."

Brynne had talked after her reconnaissance about the two stanchions of the dam each needing two charges. Stanton knew better. There was a place on one of the stanchions a couple of metres from the top where the concrete was crumbling and there was a hole you could get your fist in and pull out chunks of masonry—or place explosives. His father often grumbled about it, and about TransNational's slowness in going ahead with the new dam, saying there'd be a time soon when the stanchion would be unsafe, and if it went, the whole dam would go with it.

One charge would do it.

As Brynne said—easy.

Easier than she thought.

With his cell phone open at the page of ingredients Stanton went in and picked up a basket. Mrs. Whittier at the check-out smiled at him. She wasn't that old—not much more than fifty, he thought—but since a fall from her bicycle two years before she'd worn a perpetual frown of anxiety and worry. She was constantly trying to put the fragments of her memory in order; while she could stack shelves and manage the cash, she searched for names all the time, even the people she saw every day, and sometimes forgot her address and telephone number. He saw her rummaging through her memory, searching for his name. Usually he supplied it, but not today.

"Good morning, er, Brian."

Good.

"Morning, Mrs. Whittier."

He set off through the rows of shelves, looking for the plumbing section. He found six varieties of drain cleaner. Which would be best? He compared the contents of each. They seemed pretty much the same. He supposed any one

would do for mak
ingredients listed.
several varieties of

Was it really th

He fell into a da
one hand and cell
at his assertion that
other way of prote
else to try. He cring
dismissal of him.
didn't want her to
to be afraid to tru
he proved he was
Brynne's acceptanc
shock but secret pri
Frame dreamed of

And it would be
seconds it would tak
and when a good ti
all he had to say wa

He took anothe
For a little over one
The store was quiet
there. Mrs. Whittie
if she remembered
wouldn't remember

He set off throug

TWEL

Stanton looked f
obviously stoppe
if Mr. Cuff and

He'd showere
his parents at the
Todd Hanley w
Junior Dill was
the mill at the sa
in early," and Ju
are. See if your

Stanton starte

His father sai
mom's worried

"That's not w
know it," said St
seem to be getti
dering if I shoul
really listening
me and that's w

"Told you w

His mother
Stanton or shall

"Go ahead," s

"He's going

Stanton stare
that. I said I wa

"Why?" said Stanton, although he knew.

"Tired of being a hypocrite. Tired of doing what TransNational says and not what I know is right, like opening the dam so I don't flood the town again."

It was starting already. Stanton had walked along Riverside Drive on the way from the hotel. The river there was over its banks and was creeping towards the road. Some people were loading their cars, others sandbagging their front doors. Someone shouted to Stanton, "Tell your dad we don't want to get flooded again." A woman, crying, carried photo albums to a car. A man was trying to entice a cat into a cage. The cat put its nose in. The man moved to slam the gate and the cat took off. Stanton thought of the cat that had been swept past him as he swam to Mrs. Caithness's cabin. He wondered what had happened to it, and if this one would also be swept away.

"It wasn't *you* who flooded the town five years ago and it won't be *you* who floods it this time," Stanton's mother said firmly. "You don't have to shoulder all the blame. Heavens, you don't have to shoulder any of the blame. It's TransNational's fault, not yours."

"I should have had the guts to quit five years ago."

She moved close to her husband and took the lapels of his jacket in her hands. "So quit now. Don't torment yourself all over again."

Stanton thought he saw tears in her eyes. She released his father's jacket and leaned against him.

"If I quit, TransNational is going to make sure I don't get another engineering job in the province," said Stanton's father. "Frank Reed told me that. Then how would we manage? What would I do?"

"I hate those bastards at TransNational," Stanton's mother spat. Her jaw was clenched so tight only her lips moved as she spoke. Stanton was shocked, as he had been earlier, by the hatred and contempt he heard in her voice. She shook her head as if shaking off her anger as she went on, "We'd manage somehow."

Stanton saw his father's eyes flicker towards him and back to his wife.

"It's me that's the problem, isn't it?" Stanton said. "It's because of what it'll cost for me to go to school."

"Not just that," his father said. "When we moved back to the house we said it was for always and I'm not about to spoil those plans by forcing us to move away because I can't find work."

An engine whined out on Mill Street. Stanton looked around through the open office door. An ATV with two riders, helmeted and with scarves over noses and mouths, a man and a woman, Stanton thought, roared into the yard and up to the office steps. The passenger hurled a rock at the office window. Stanton and his parents turned away covering their faces as it shattered. The driver shouted, "We know where you live, Frame, and it'll be your house next if you don't open the dam."

Les, Todd, and Junior were running across the yard.

Junior called, "Everyone all right?"

The ATV, spitting gravel, roared out of the yard and up Mill Street.

"No damage," replied Stanton's father. "Not to us, anyway."

"Call Sergeant Munn," said Les. "Todd and me'll go after them."

"Let 'em go," said Stanton's father. "They're long gone already, anyway, and there's no way Ernie's going to trace who they are."

The men moved away, talking quietly.

Stanton's mother said, "It's time to quit and get out of here, Willis. Why don't you do it? Why don't you do it—right now?"

"And leave the town to the mercy of TransNational?" said Stanton's father. "No. If I quit, I'll make sure the dam's open before I go."

"The company won't let you open the dam. You'd never even get the gate crew together without Junior knowing and reporting you, and it'd be shut in no time."

"There's more than one way to open the gates," said Stanton's father. "And keep them open."

His wife stared at him.

Stanton was about to ask if he meant what he thought he meant when his phone rang and Jessica said, "Get yourself down to the green. Blaine Tupper's arriving at noon."

Stanton glanced at his watch. It was 11:55. "Blaine Tupper the premier?"

"No. Blaine Tupper the tooth fairy. Of course the premier."

"How come no one knows?"

"'Cause no one knows. It's been kept secret because his security guys got wind there are agitators in town and there's going to be a demonstration of some kind about the dam."

Stanton thought, *Agitators like Callie and Brynne.* "Is there?"

"Not that I've heard. He's coming by helicopter. Landing on the green and making a speech on the town hall steps about the good job TransNational's doing keeping the town safe from flooding. Then touring the mill."

"How come you know all this?"

"Callie got a call."

"Who from?"

"Don't know. Probably EcoAction headquarters."

"How would they know?"

"Told you before. EcoAction has informers."

"In the *premier's* office?"

"Guess so. All I know is someone called Callie and she told me. Hurry now." She ended the call. Stanton's parents had been listening.

"What's going on?" his father asked.

"Premier's visiting town and making a speech and touring the mill. Arriving in a few minutes."

"*What?*"

The phone in the office rang. Stanton's father picked it up and listened. He looked at Stanton. "Okay, Frank. Thank you." He put the phone down. "That was Frank Reed, saying the premier's paying us a surprise visit. How the hell did you know?"

"Callie got a call about it. Someone in the premier's office tipped off EcoAction."

His father said incredulously, "The premier's visiting the place I'm responsible for and your friends know about it before I do? Just who are these young women?"

"Like they said at the meeting—EcoAction has informers," said Stanton. "I'm going to the green."

"Before you go...."

Stanton stopped in the doorway.

"I know how you feel about Jessica and I understand it because she's a fine girl and you know I agree with much of what she says about the environment and TransNational and all that, although I'm not supposed to say so. But I don't trust the outfit she's got herself involved with, and I don't trust Callie and Brynne. I'm afraid they're trouble, and I don't want you and Jessica getting sucked into it."

Stanton's mother added, "Take care, dear."

Stanton said, "Don't worry."

Yesterday it was Jessica telling me not to worry, he thought. *Now I'm telling my folks the same thing.*

As he left the office his eye fell on the storage shed where his father kept the explosives he'd been trained to use for an ice jam. He wondered suddenly, remembering his father's comment about there being more than one way to open the gates and keep them open, if his anger would really drive him—allow him—to go as far as destroying the place he'd worked at for over twenty years.

A van pulled into the yard. Twelve security guards with helmets and shields and batons jumped out and arranged themselves across the entrance.

Stanton's father ran from the office. "What's all this?"

"TransNational's head office sent us to supplement the premier's security arrangements during his tour of the mill," said their chief. "Just a precaution, sir."

It was noon. Twelve hours to flood time.

THIRTEEN

The green was cordoned off by men in dark suits and sunglasses who stood around its perimeter. Stanton found Jessica among the crowd gathering where Main Street ran alongside the green, attracted by the security detail and the distant clatter of a helicopter. Sergeant Munn, Dave Watson, and three officers Stanton didn't know stood nearby. Fred Shingles prowled back and forth on the edge of the crowd. Callie and Brynne stood with half a dozen strangers, four men and two women.

"Reinforcements from EcoAction?" Stanton murmured.

Jessica nodded. "They got here late last night. They're camping outside town."

The sound grew louder and a helicopter swooped over the Presbyterian church, circled the green twice, and hovered for a few seconds before descending beside the town hall. As the rotors slowed the security detail reformed around it.

The premier emerged and walked towards the wide steps of the town hall. A man and a woman Stanton took for aides walked half a step behind him, followed by three men and two women, all business-suited. Stanton recognized Frank Reed and guessed the others were also TransNational executives. At the same time the doors of the town hall opened and Verna Mullen appeared, flanked by eight town councillors. They stood on the top step, where a microphone had been set up. The premier, a short, strutting man with grey hair slicked across his head and a thin grey-black moustache, led his entourage up the steps and along the line of councillors, shaking hands as he went, before taking his place beside the mayor.

Meanwhile the security detail had moved into a wide semicircle along a roped-off enclosure around the town hall steps. The crowd moved forward. Sergeant Munn and the other officers stood beside the single entrance to the enclosure, watching people as they filed through. Fred Shingles approached. Sergeant Munn moved in front of him and shook his head. "Sorry, Fred. Best listen from out here."

"Are we living in a fascist state now? I've got every right—"

"Don't push your luck, Fred. Especially after what happened when Dave tried to help you this morning."

Shingles stepped back, muttering to himself.

Jessica and Stanton approached together. Stanton stood back to let Jessica go first. Sergeant Munn took half a step across the entrance, looking hard at her. He stepped back and said quietly, "Okay, Jess. You too, Stanton." He looked at Callie and Brynne and the newcomers from EcoAction, who waited behind Stanton, and added, "But not your friends, I'm afraid."

"Welcome to the police state of Black River," one of them said loudly.

Another added, "You got no right to stop us."

"I do have the right," said Sergeant Munn. "But you're welcome to listen from there."

Jessica and Stanton, already inside the enclosure, left and stood with the EcoAction group.

"Guess you don't like strangers in Black River," one of the newcomers told Sergeant Munn.

"Or are you afraid of them?" another taunted.

"It's just a precaution for everyone's good, including yours. I apologize for the inconvenience," said Sergeant Munn.

Someone in the EcoAction crowd muttered, "Pig."

Sergeant Munn took no notice.

Stanton felt sorry for him.

When all the crowd was inside the cordon, except Stanton, Jessica, Fred Shingles, and the EcoAction contingent, Verna Mullen said into the microphone, "In Black River's time of need, we can always count on two things, the support of our own TransNational Power, and of our premier, the Honourable Blaine Tupper."

As soon as the mayor started talking, Sergeant Munn and the rest of the police stood across the entrance to the roped-off area, closing it, so that as newcomers arrived, drawn by the helicopter and the amplified voice, they joined the EcoAction contingent, forming a growing audience of excluded listeners.

"As you know, for the last few days the good people at TransNational have been working day and night to alleviate the risk of flooding," Verna Mullen went on.

"Hogwash!" Fred Shingles shouted.

"Why don't they just open the dam?" a newcomer to the crowd outside the enclosure called.

Verna Mullen kept going. "Now, at a time when our community is under duress, stricken with anxiety as it faces the risk of another flood, it is my pleasure to welcome Premier Tupper to Black River. We are confident that with his help and support, and with the ongoing help and support of TransNational Power—"

"Who are flooding the town!" shouted Callie.

Vera Mullen stumbled on. "With the help and support of the premier and TransNational Power we can deal with whatever trials the next few hours and days bring, and emerge stronger and more resilient than ever."

Fred Shingles, standing beside Stanton and Jessica at the front of the excluded crowd, commented loudly, "Can you believe this bullshit?"

Sergeant Munn warned, "Language, Fred."

"Please join me in welcoming the Honourable Blaine Tupper," the mayor concluded.

As a few people within the enclosure clapped, Blaine Tupper shook hands with Verna Mullen again before taking his place at the microphone.

"Mayor Mullen, councillors, executives of TransNational Power, and townspeople of Black River: I come to you on behalf not just of my government, but of the entire province, with the promise that we will do all we can to prevent your town being flooded, at the same time as we prudently prepare for the consequences of flood by implementing rescue and care procedures through our Emergency Measures Organization. This includes the provision of a shelter for flood victims, already open at the Community Centre on Main Street, and mechanisms by which flood victims can file for compensation, as well as find help and advice on what to do in the event of flood. In addition, TransNational Power has pledged to pay the amount of...." Blaine Tupper paused and looked around at his audience. "One thousand dollars—yes, *one thousand* dollars—to each and every flood victim, despite the company having no responsibility for any flooding that may occur."

"Only after they sign a paper promising they won't make any further claim against TransNational even if they find the damage comes to more than that!" one of the EcoAction newcomers yelled.

"That's not true," said the premier confidently.

"Why don't you ask the TransNational guys beside you?" the heckler retorted.

Blaine Tupper looked uncertainly at the TransNational executives. Frank Reed rose and spoke quietly to him, and the premier turned back to the microphone. "I am told a signature is required simply to cover liability issues."

"You bet it is," scoffed the heckler.

"And TransNational's thousand dollars is nothing but a spit in the bucket anyway," one of the townspeople who had joined the crowd outside the rope added.

Sergeant Munn signalled to the police to fan out and face the crowd outside the enclosure.

"Trying to frighten us, Ernie?" a woman taunted.

The excluded group was growing as more people walked across the green from Main Street and motorists driving alongside the green stopped and left their cars to listen.

"Let me share a few facts with you that the good people at TransNational Power are too modest to reveal themselves," said Blaine Tupper.

"Like how many thousand acres of farmland they flooded in Manitoba last year," one of the EcoAction contingent shouted.

The premier continued. "Their contribution to the provincial economy through taxes stands at five million dollars—five *million* dollars!—not to mention the generous wages they pay to their five hundred employees in the province, and the contribution those wages make to the local and provincial economy. In fact, TransNational Power is the single biggest contributor to the provincial economy—"

"And the single biggest destroyer of the environment," Jessica called out.

"And one without which the province would be in dire financial straits. The company is also a generous annual contributor to the United Way and to countless individual causes that it supports in dozens of communities, one of them Black River, including causes that could not survive without their help. Charities like Every Kid a Reader, food banks, and Treats for Sick Kids.

"Bearing all this in mind, we thank TransNational for having the confidence to keep the dam closed—which, as you know, has no effect on water levels—so the generation of power can continue at maximum efficiency, ensuring the comfort and financial well-being of your community and of the province. To show our gratitude for its careful stewardship of the Black River, and for its contribution to town and province, the mayor and I will now tour the dam. But before we do, I invite you to join me in thanking TransNational Power in the traditional way!"

He held his hands apart, as if about to applaud, cueing his audience to follow.

One of the aides clapped twice, stopped, gestured to the other aide to join in, and started clapping again. The premier and Verna Mullen and two councillors joined in. A few people among the crowd inside the enclosure started to clap, looked around, and stopped. No one outside the enclosure applauded.

The premier held up his hands and roared, with a rising inflection, as if he was a rock star at a stadium concert, "Thank you, Black River!"

One of the TransNational executives had moved out of the line of dignitaries to talk on his cell. Now he approached Blaine Tupper, who covered the microphone with his hand as the executive whispered to him. The premier smiled broadly and turned back to the microphone. "I have just received good news! It comes from our friends at TransNational, whose tireless engineers have for the last few days been feeding all available information into a specially developed computer program and who have just sent word that they are now confident the Black River crested two hours ago, at ten o'clock this morning. In other words…" He looked around at the crowd, smiling, before adding, "The danger of flood has passed!"

There was a beat of silence.

Then Callie shouted, "Bullshit!"

"It's already over its banks on Riverside, you jerk," someone from the crowd inside the enclosure yelled.

"And it's been over its banks for the last few days upriver," a man behind Stanton added.

"TransNational flooded the town five years ago and they're doing it again—right now!" another called.

Fred Shingles roared, "TransNational doesn't know shit about the river!"

Sergeant Munn said sharply, "Fred, that's enough."

Shingles kept shouting. "We, the people of Black River, we're the ones who know the river. You people at TransNational think you know all about it and think you can do what you like with it because you think you own it, but I got news for you. You don't own it! You know why? Because we do! We, the people, we own the river!"

Sergeant Munn ordered Dave Watson, "Get him out of here."

It was too late. The crowd outside the cordon, now twenty or thirty strong and led by the EcoAction contingent, swarmed around Shingles, preventing Dave Watson from reaching him. At the same time they took up the chant.

"We own the river!"

Brynne shouted, "March on the dam!" and the crowd set off across the green, the EcoAction contingent and the rest of the protestors close behind.

Dave Watson looked at Sergeant Munn, who said, "The premier."

Stanton, about to follow Jessica, who was already marching and chanting with the crowd, stopped and looked around. The people from inside the cordon had climbed the steps and surrounded the premier and the mayor and, with the councillors, were chanting in their faces, "We own the river."

The security detail abandoned their posts around the enclosure and, with Sergeant Munn and his police, pushed through the crowd on the steps and formed a new cordon, this one around Blaine Tupper and Verna Mullen. As soon as the premier and the mayor were shielded by the security detail, the crowd lost interest in them and hurried to join the group following Shingles, now on the other side of the green and setting off up Main Street, heading for Mill Street.

Stanton, listening to the chant as he ran to catch up with Jessica, wondered when ownership of the river became an issue. From what he knew of the history of the town, it seemed no one had asked who owned the river when the old Black River Pulp and Paper Company started using it to power its saws and grinders in 1899. Neither did the question of ownership arise when Black River Power took over the mill. The use of the river's power still seemed the natural thing to do, and didn't affect its flow or the level of its waters. But something changed when TransNational took over, something to do with the arrogance of power that allowed the company to disregard the natural state of the river, to put commerce above the well-being of the community, and to end the harmonious relationship between the river and its use by the mill, use of the river turning to abuse.

Jessica, already on the other side of the green, was marching between Callie and Brynne. As Stanton got closer, he saw the two girls and the rest of the EcoAction band pull black balaclavas over their heads. Suddenly they'd transformed into anonymous, menacing figures of anarchy and mayhem. With the lead of the EcoAction band, the chant changed from "We own the river!" to "Take back the river—open the dam!"

Stanton pulled out his cell and dialled as he ran. "Dad, they're coming. They're marching on the mill. They're going to try and open the dam!"

On the other side of the green, the premier and his aides still huddled in the centre of the security detail, while Verna Mullen fled into the town hall. The helicopter's rotors were turning slowly. Sergeant Munn pointed the premier towards it. Bending low, Blaine Tupper and his entourage scuttled over and climbed in. As the rotors increased speed, Sergeant Munn and the police set off across the green.

Meanwhile the march was growing as people spilled from stores and joined it on its way along Main Street. At the corner of Main and Mill Street, the marchers paused and fell silent, contemplating the gates of the mill just ahead, past Black River Java. Then it proceeded in a silence that to Stanton seemed more menacing than the chanting, as if the crowd was now less intent on sending a message and more intent on wreaking destruction.

The protesters stopped at the two-metre wire mesh of the closed gates.

The security guards, shields and batons at the ready, stood in a row across and behind the entrance gates.

The black hooded figures, who had been scattered among the marchers, moved to the front and one told Shingles,

"Stand back, Mr. Shingles. We're used to this." They stared at the guards, who stared back, their eyes invisible behind the visors of their helmets.

Then, at some unseen signal, the guards roared a guttural, feral grunt, slamming their batons against their shields, before falling back into silence. Their leader was speaking urgently into a radio.

The marchers fell back a few steps, except the EcoAction band, who pushed against the gates, fingers curled around the wire. Two of the EcoAction marchers, one on each side of the gates, started to scale the wire while their comrades started pushing and pulling the gates, so that the crowd fell back as they heaved them outwards then surged forward as they sent them bulging inwards.

Through the gates Stanton, caught up in the advancing and retreating movement of the crowd, saw his father and mother through the open door of the office, huddled with Junior, Les, and Todd. He glimpsed Jessica near the front of the marchers but couldn't get to her.

As the to and fro rocking motion intensified, the EcoAction marchers who were scaling the gates reached the top and straddled them like rodeo riders. They punched the air, urging the crowd onwards with each forward surge, until suddenly the gates gave way. The guards were sent scrambling backwards until they reformed into a new line halfway between the entrance to the yard and the dam itself.

The guards at each end of the line grappled with the EcoAction climbers, who had jumped on them as the gates collapsed. One of the climbers went down at a single swing of the guard's baton, while on the other side an EcoAction protester ran to help his comrade, jumping the guard from behind and pulling him to the ground.

Junior ran from the office, shaking his fist at the marchers and shouting at the guards, "Get this mob out of the yard!"

The helicopter, rising from the green, clattered overhead, causing a brief lull as guards and marchers looked up as if expecting aerial intervention.

In the quiet, Stanton heard the guards' leader tell Junior, "Stay in the office with the others, please, sir, and let us do our job. Reinforcements are on the way."

Stanton heard sirens in the distance. Junior ignored the order and assumed a place in the line of guards, which started advancing slowly, eyes fixed on the crowd.

Stanton glimpsed Jessica in the middle of the EcoAction band, still between Callie and Brynne. He wanted to shout to her to wait for him but knew she wouldn't hear him over the clatter of the departing helicopter, the whoop of sirens getting closer, the noise of the river, and the rhythmic slamming of batons against shields by the guards as they advanced on the crowd. Trying to fight his way towards Jessica, he saw his father and mother staring from the office.

When the crowd and the guards were just a few metres apart, the crowd hesitated, then stopped. The guards kept moving, beating their shields with their batons as they advanced with small, slow steps, still uttering their fierce, animal-like grunt every few paces. Stanton pushed his way past a few more people and had nearly reached Jessica when the line of guards stopped with a final grunt and slam of baton on shield.

The sirens were growing louder all the time. The protesters and the guards faced one another. Stanton heard uneasy murmurs from the people around him:

"Enough of this."

"I don't like how this is going."

The guards' chief barked at the crowd, "All of you, fall back now, before police reinforcements arrive, or you will be charged with disorderly conduct and hindering security guards in the course of their duty."

An EcoAction protester walked up to one of the guards with his arms held wide in a gesture of peace and reconciliation. The guard relaxed his hold on his shield and baton. Another EcoAction protester darted from the crowd, circled behind, and suddenly the guard was on the ground. The guard beside him rushed to help. Callie ran forward and tripped him and he fell. Another guard seized her from behind and held her with his shield under her chin, forcing her head back.

For a few seconds Stanton was shocked a guard could so violently hold a girl hardly older than Jessica. Then he realized gender had become irrelevant. All that mattered now was whose side you were on. He looked for Jessica again as one of the EcoAction band shouted, "Charge!" and the crowd surged forward.

Looking around, he glimpsed his father and mother still at the open office door. Les and Todd were holding his father back. Recalling his father's threat only an hour before to quit TransNational and open the dam and make sure it stayed open, Stanton wondered if his father's workmates were stopping him from opposing the protesters, or joining them.

At the same time he asked himself, *So whose side am I on? Am I with Jessica and her new friends and the protesters? Or am I with Dad, wherever his allegiances now lie?*

Fred Shingles was shouting in a guard's face, spittle flying. The guard held his baton at both ends and whipped it upwards, catching Shingles under the nose. Blood ran down his face as he reeled backwards. He gathered himself and lunged at the guard, who lashed his baton at Shingles's shoulder. Shingles ducked and the baton caught him across the face.

Brynne circled behind the guard holding Callie and swept his feet from under him. Callie kicked him as he fell. He scrambled up and laid two quick blows on her with his baton, elbow and chin, as another guard struck Brynne on the back of her neck with his baton. She turned. The guard went to swing again, but Brynne leaned back, raised one long, elegant leg, and smashed her boot on his chin. She did it with such ease and grace, Stanton wondered if some kind of martial arts training came with joining EcoAction. He was embarrassingly aware that he could never pull off a move like that. All he knew was what his father had taught him when he found himself the target of bullying in grade four.

The guard staggered back and Brynne kicked again, the side of his knee this time. He gasped and toppled over. Another guard grabbed her from behind, both arms around her. She slithered out of his grasp and swung around to advance on him. Callie, holding her arms up to shield her face, was retreating before a rain of blows from the guard she'd tripped.

Stanton watched the skirmishes all around him, action stymied not just by doubt about where he belonged but also by his father's teaching him to get in a fight only if he absolutely had to because, he said, there was no winner in a fight, only the pity of being dragged into uncivilized behaviour. There was also the fear, Stanton had to admit, that he would be easily overpowered by the guards if he joined the mêlée, and would be shamed and humiliated in front of everyone, including Jessica, Brynne, and Callie, while Brynne flattened the guards with ease.

One of his high school teachers was yelling in a guard's face. A town councillor was locked in a shoving match with another. Tess and one of her customers, who'd joined the marchers as they passed Black River Java, were flailing at a guard as he propelled them backwards with his shield. Then Jessica burst from the crowd and ran to help Callie, who was falling backwards, still trying to cover her head as the guard swung his baton repeatedly. Junior left his place in the line of guards and darted in front of Jessica, holding his forearm high so her face smacked into it.

And suddenly it didn't matter to Stanton where he belonged, because now the decision to act was personal.

Blood was spurting from Jessica's nose as she fell. She started to push herself up but Junior slapped her and she dropped to the ground again. Stanton remembered his father telling him, "You get in a fight only to defend yourself or a friend. And then forget the fancy moves you see on TV shows, and forget any notion of rules or of what is acceptable in a fight, because there are no rules. So you poke your attacker in the eyes. You shove two fingers up his nose as hard as you can. You punch him in the throat. And of course you kick him or knee him in the balls. Remember: eyes, nose, throat, balls."

Stanton, shoving guards and protesters aside as he moved towards Jessica, heard Junior growl at her, "You're the cause of this, stirring up trouble, bringing strangers to town who've got no business here." Fleetingly, as he elbowed a guard aside on his way to Jessica, Stanton puzzled over the resentment and rage Junior was levelling at her. He wondered where it came from, but at the same time felt a curious pride in her, that Junior was singling her out for such anger, as if she were the leader of the opposition to the dam.

Junior had taken her chin between thumb and fingers and was squeezing hard and shaking her head violently backwards and forwards as Stanton arrived at a run, shoving aside the last two people between him and Jessica, not knowing or caring whether they were protesters or guards. He swung a carefully aimed kick. His foot shot between Jessica and Junior Dill and smashed into Junior's throat.

Junior released Jessica and reeled backwards, clutching his throat and gagging. Stanton grabbed him by his jacket, pulled him towards him, and thrust two fingers in his eyes. Junior gasped and his hands flew to his face. Stanton stepped close to him and brought his knee up hard between Junior's legs. As Junior doubled up, Stanton swung his fist upwards into his face where it landed on his nose with a liquid smack. Junior dropped at Stanton's feet.

At the same time the crowd, now only a few metres from the dam and close behind two members of EcoAction who were about to climb on it, stopped its advance.

Stanton was aware of a still, silent centre in the fray where marchers and guards stood in a circle. The stillness and quiet spread outward through the crowd and the guards, like a widening ripple in a lake, stopping the scuffles and shouting matches going on all around the yard.

Sergeant Munn and Dave Watson were pushing through the crowd, their colleagues behind them. The sirens grew louder and stopped and car doors slammed. Sergeant Munn stopped at the hushed, unmoving centre of the crowd and told Dave Watson, "Ambulance."

He knelt beside Fred Shingles, who lay motionless with eyes closed, his body at a curious angle, half on his side but his head and shoulders twisted the other way, one arm flung sideways, the other trapped under him. Blood ran from a cut over his eye and from his nose and pooled on the ground beside him. A guard standing uncertainly over him repeated to anyone who'd listen, "He must have fallen and hit his head."

Stanton's father ran from the office with Les and Todd. His mother hovered in the doorway.

Stanton had never been in a fight before, not a real one, only minor playground scuffles and a few brief skirmishes in rugby and hockey games. Nothing like this. He looked down at Junior, waiting to feel some kind of thrill of victory, or at least some satisfaction at revenging his attack on Jessica. But the best Stanton could come up with, as Junior raised his head and stared at him, was a kind of guilty triumph. His father was right: there was no winner in a fight.

Shingles stirred and muttered something.

Sergeant Munn said, "Lie still, Fred. Help's on the way."

Stanton knelt beside Jessica. She pushed herself to a sitting position. "Are you okay?" Stanton asked.

"What the fuck does it look like?" she said as she wiped blood from her nose with her sleeve. There was a raw red welt on her face where Junior had slapped her.

Sergeant Munn put his hand on Shingles's shoulder to hold him still. Shingles batted it away and struggled up. He looked slowly around at the marchers and guards surrounding him until he saw Stanton's father and Junior and growled, "I'll have revenge on you and TransNational for setting the guards on me. And for assaulting me. And for flooding my home and my town."

Holding his arm awkwardly across his chest, he started for the gate, blood dripping down his face and leaving a trail in the dust. The crowd parted for him.

Sergeant Munn called after him, "Fred, I wish you'd wait for the ambulance."

Shingles tottered through the marchers and guards, muttering, "You don't know what you've started. I got friends a phone call away gonna love coming up here and teaching TransNational a lesson." He turned and shook his fist and shouted, "Now it's all-out war!"

Three police cruisers were parked across the entrance to the yard, lights flashing. One of the officers who had arrived moved to stop Shingles as he shuffled on, but Sergeant Munn called, "Leave him be."

Two ambulances arrived, sirens wailing.

Jessica stood uncertainly. Stanton put his arm round her shoulders to steady her. "Where are Callie and Brynne? Are they okay?" she asked.

Stanton looked around. There was no sign of them or any of the EcoAction band. They had disappeared within a few minutes of the mêlée ending.

Sergeant Munn said, "Paramedics are here, Jess. Let them take a look at you."

She stared around until her eyes fell on Stanton's father and Junior Dill, who was pulling himself to his feet.

She spat, "You have no idea what you've brought down on yourselves."

FOURTEEN

For a few seconds Stanton and Jessica were alone in the middle of the quickly emptying mill yard.

The last few demonstrators were walking away on Mill Street. Sergeant Munn was huddled at the gate with Stanton's father and the police. Stanton's mother stood a short distance away. The security guards were loading their van and the ambulances were moving out. Junior, with a final glare at Stanton, had stalked out onto the dam, muttering about checking for damage. Les and Todd joined him.

Stanton put both arms around Jessica and pulled her close. Her nostrils were stuffed with cotton wool. The paramedics, after making sure her nose was not broken, said it was all they could do for her. For a few seconds he felt her tense and unyielding against him, then she relaxed slightly and rested her head on his shoulder. Blood had congealed and dried under her nose, her cheek was still inflamed where Junior had slapped her, and her chin was bruised on one side where his thumb had dug into her skin. Stanton could feel her shaking and tightened his arms around her as if he could stop it.

"Holy shit I didn't think it would be like that," she muttered. Stanton patted her back, trying to comfort her, and she said, "I'm not a fucking dog."

Stanton's parents joined them. His mother hugged first Stanton, then Jessica.

His father said, "You and Jess okay?"

Stanton mumbled, "Sorry."

"For what?"

"Assaulting Mr. Dill."

"He asked for it, going at Jess like that. I should have done it myself."

"And sorry for going against you."

"Going against me—how?"

"Siding with EcoAction and the others against the company."

"I wanted to join you. That's why Les and Todd were holding me. Said it was for my own good. You and Jess and your EcoAction friends are on the right side."

Stanton's mother offered to clean up Jessica's face in the office, and to hide her bruises with some makeup, but she said she had to get back to her grandmother. Stanton's father told him to get the car from the hotel and drive Jessica out to the lake.

As they set off up Mill Street, they heard a quiet "Hey!" Callie beckoned from the Black River Java drive-through. She backed away towards the car park at the rear of the coffee shop. Stanton and Jessica followed. Brynne and the rest of the EcoAction band, without balaclavas now, lurked between the dumpster and the lattice-screened patio.

Callie took Jessica's face between her hands. "You okay?"

"Couple of bruises. You?"

"Sore chin and stiff elbow. I've had worse."

"Let's get a coffee."

"Best we keep out of sight. Anyway, we've got to keep moving. Get packed up. We're getting the early bus tomorrow."

"Where to?"

"Anywhere out of town. Then we'll check in with HQ. See if they want us to do anything more here or join the action somewhere else. If there's nothing, Brynne and me will be heading back to BC."

"How d'you think it went?"

"The demo? We stopped the premier visiting the mill. That'll piss the company off. Show them we've got a bit of muscle, can influence things. What d'you think? Did you get your message across to TransNational?"

"Think so."

"Will they listen? Change how they act?"

"Probably not."

"That's why you keep the pressure on. Get right in their face like we just did—and stay there. It's not over yet."

Brynne said, "Better move on. Lot of police around."

Callie hugged Jessica. "Keep the faith."

Stanton had been standing back.

Callie offered him her hand. "Must be hard going against your dad."

Stanton nodded and took her hand.

She added, "Sorry we didn't trust you at first. It's how you get in this game."

"This way," Brynne instructed the group. "Then split. Keep your heads down. Meet at the campsite in one hour."

She nodded to Jessica and Stanton, and the EcoAction band raised their hands in a salute. Then Brynne led them across a garden that bordered the Black River Java car park and out onto a quiet lane which led out of town. Stanton and Jessica, looking across the garden, watched as the group broke up and moved briskly off in different directions. Within seconds they'd disappeared.

They went into Black River Java. They were the only customers. Tess was already back at work. She brought them coffee. "On the house for fellow protesters."

They took the table in the window where they'd sat with Callie and Brynne. When Jessica reached for her cup Stanton saw her hand was trembling and he laid his over it, but she pulled away.

He said, "Are you mad at me for something?"

"I just don't understand you."

"Like how?"

"Like first you say you don't believe in direct action. Then you beat the crap out of Junior Dill."

"I did it for you; he was assaulting you."

"I know. It's just—" She started to cry. "—it's just I didn't think it would be like that. It's like it turned you into someone I don't know."

Stanton thought bitterly, *And someone you don't like. I suppose you'd rather I stood aside and let Junior beat you up.*

His father's words came back to him again: no one wins a fight. It seemed like he would be a loser twice over, in throwing aside his principles by fighting, and by creating this distance from Jessica. He thought she would admire him for his actions and be pleased by the way he aligned himself with her and her EcoAction friends.

In an effort to deflect her thoughts from him, he said, "You mean you didn't think protesting would turn violent like that?" He wanted to add, *So what did you expect, the way Callie and Brynne were talking?*

She nodded. "Who—what—started it, anyway?"

"What set things off was the EcoAction people jumping on the security guards from on top of the gates, but it could have been anything or anyone. Depends how far back you want to go, I guess. Basically, TransNational started it, by not opening the dam."

"Hope what you did doesn't set you too much against your dad."

"You heard what he said. He's more on our side than the company's."

"But the protest didn't really do any good, did it? The dam's still closed, and Grandma's cabin is still going to be flooded in a few hours." She glanced at her watch. It was four thirty. "In seven and a half hours, to be precise."

"Maybe TransNational got the message. Maybe they'll open it now."

Jessica rolled her eyes. "Yeah. And maybe there really is a Santa Claus."

They waved to Tess and walked out onto Mill Street. A police car drove from the mill yard. Jessica watched it.

"But like Callie said: it's not over yet."

"What d'you mean?"

"Just—it's not over."

They set off for the hotel to get the car. It was like a Sunday morning on Main, when Stanton's father liked to say you could safely fire a cannon down the street. Carmichael's and the liquor store were closed. A Red Cross van was parked at the community centre but there was no sign of activity. Stanton wondered if people were hiding out, shocked by the violence at the mill. Maybe they were afraid of the consequences of their being part of it. Maybe ashamed.

Was he?

He didn't think so, not completely, despite what Jessica said. He was proud of acting against TransNational even if it was late, kind of by accident, and forced by Junior's attack on Jessica. But suppose he'd come on the scene like the people who drifted across the green, drawn by the helicopter's arrival and the speeches. Would he have joined the march then? Or was it just Jessica's involvement that got him involved?

At the hotel, they lay side by side on the bed in Stanton's room for an hour, holding hands and watching TV, not speaking. Then they drove to the lake and parked for a while. He cautiously put his arm around her shoulders and was pleased when she leaned across the seat and curled herself against him.

They sat in silence until she asked, "What are you going to do?"

"Check in with my folks. I want to talk to Dad...."

"I mean—what are you really going to do, when you finish school? Like, what are you going to do with your life?"

"What brought that on?"

"Just thinking about all the stuff that's happened the last few days."

"Study engineering. You know that."

"Then what?"

"Depends what comes up. I'm not like you, on a fixed course, driven by conviction and belief. I wish I was."

"If I got involved with an environmental organization, maybe something like EcoAction, would you work with me?"

"Sure."

"Would you commit to direct action"—she looked at him with a wry grin—"now you've got a taste for it?"

He hesitated. Said cautiously, "Maybe."

"That's what you said before—remember?"

He remembered.

Jessica pressed. "You're still not sure about it, are you? Not totally committed."

"Committed—like, how?"

"You know what I mean. Only reason you got into the action today was because of Junior. But you're still not totally committed to doing whatever it takes, including direct action—like, extreme action—to stop outfits like TransNational destroying the environment."

He said quietly, "No." It felt like a confession, and he added, "Sorry."

Jessica said sadly, "Me, too."

They sat in silence for a few seconds. Then Jessica said, "I better go."

"Hope you and your grandma will be all right with the flood coming."

"We'll manage."

"See you tomorrow sometime, then."

She climbed from the car. He got out and ran to the dock ahead of her, untied the boat and held it while she climbed in. It pitched and heaved against his grasp in the high, choppy water of the lake. She clung to the sides and leaned forward to kiss him, then held him with her eyes for a long time.

He said, "Now what?"

She shook her head. "Nothing."

She started the motor and blew him a kiss as he pushed the boat clear of the ramp. She turned the boat and opened the throttle and headed for the point. She looked back and said something but he couldn't hear above the noise of the motor. He shouted, "What?" but she was looking towards the point and didn't seem to hear. She didn't look back again.

He was still sitting by the lake, watching the wake of Jessica's boat spread into oblivion, when his phone rang. It was his mother.

"As if we haven't got enough to worry about already," she said, "now your Aunt Jodie's been taken to hospital. The usual stuff, but worse than usual. She thought she'd got it under control but it flared up again and she's in a bad way. She called from Lewisport General. I have to go and see her. She's got no one else."

"I'm at the lake," he said. "I'll have the car to you in a few minutes."

"No need. I'm already at the bus station, and the bus is about to leave. It's only a couple of hours to Lewisport. Besides, your dad's going to need the car with all the trouble, and he'll likely need to go to the head office. Sergeant Munn was still talking to him when Jodie called, and Frank Reed's coming down. He wants to have supper and talk things over and your dad's in a state worrying about that, of course, so I didn't tell him about Jodie because I didn't want to bother him with her problems, just told him I'd see him later. Would you tell him, please, and say not to call me because I'll be at the hospital, and I'll call in the morning?"

"Okay."

"And try and get him not to worry."

"Yeah, right."

Stanton drove back to town and left the car at the hotel. He walked to the mill hoping to see his father, but there were still police at the gates and patrolling the grounds. He spotted his father with Sergeant Munn and Junior in the office talking, so he turned away.

He wandered aimlessly around town, which was still unusually quiet. He stopped in at Black River Java for a bowl of soup and a coffee for supper. He was the only customer again and Tess sat with him. She said her parents had already moved out of their house and were staying at the emergency shelter because they didn't want to be driven out in the middle of the night.

"How about you?" she asked. "Are you staying up all night to watch the flood?"

"Dunno. I'm still at the hotel so I'll see what Dad does."

"Is Jess there, too?"

"Nah. She's staying out at the lake with her grandma."

"Seems strange, seeing you without her. It's like you're always together. I saw how you took Junior down when he attacked her, like you're her guardian angel."

"Don't know how I feel about slugging him like that," Stanton confessed.

"Well, don't feel bad, for heaven's sake," said Tess. "He was right out of line, going at Jess like he did."

"Strange how he seemed so mad at her," said Stanton. "Like he was out of control he was so angry."

"He wasn't attacking Jess," she said. "He was attacking his wife."

"What d'you mean?"

"Don't you know? He's mad at women in general, ever since his wife found a new man and walked out on him. He's always looking for someone, preferably female, to take it out on. He tried getting mad at me one day when I was slow getting his coffee." She grinned. "But he only tried it once."

"I don't follow the town gossip."

"You can't help hearing it, working here."

Stanton drained his coffee and stood. "I better get back to the hotel. See if Dad's there."

"Make sure you come back," said Tess. "Come in when it's quiet so we have time to sit and chat."

Back at the hotel, Stanton stayed awake as long as he could then left a note for his father saying Aunt Jodie was in hospital and that his mom had caught the bus to Lewisport to be with her.

He wondered if Jessica and Mrs. Caithness had gone to bed in the attic, or if they were sitting up, waiting for the lake to run through the cabin. He thought of Jessica's disappointment in him, at his failure to share her conviction that taking extreme action to right environmental wrongs was always justified. He wished he'd lied and said he was committed to it. It would have been easier than facing her disappointment.

The last time he looked at the clock before he fell asleep it was eleven thirty. Half an hour to flood time.

FIFTEEN

When it came, he could not say it was unexpected.

The sharp crack followed by the dull roar, like a distant rumble of thunder, or an ice jam breaking up.

A moment of stillness and silence.

Then the easy disintegration and tumble of the weakest stanchion, already undermined by its flaking mortar. The slow crumbling and collapse down the falls of the second stanchion, the stronger one, resisting longer but fatally damaged, weakened by the blast and finished off by the force of thousands of tons of water suddenly released. The iron frames followed, leaving the dam an astonishing, gaping, jagged-toothed hole.

Stanton's phone was ringing.

He thought he'd been awake.

He looked at the bedside clock.

Who would call at three o'clock in the morning?

His mother, from the hospital. Something must've happened with Aunt Jodie. Something serious.

No, she'd call his father.

Jessica, then. Had to be. In trouble at the lake. Trapped with her grandmother in the loft, the lake roaring through the cabin, threatening to sweep it away.

He groped in the dark for his phone.

Another roar, more prolonged this time. That definitely wasn't a dream.

It sounded as if the logs released, rolling and crashing and cartwheeling end over end down the falls and careening through the gorge, slowing only when they entered the calmer salt water of the estuary. At last the smooth sweep and roil of the river pouring where the dam had been, the river and gorge returned to their natural state, before the machinations of Black River Pulp and Paper, and Black River Power, and TransNational Power.

His phone stopped ringing.

The door of the adjoining room opened and closed. Footsteps crossed the room and there was a knock.

His father looked around the door of Stanton's room. "Are you awake? I heard something. An explosion, I think. At the mill."

"I heard something too. Thought I was dreaming."

"The threats, you know. I was on the way to check. Came back to tell you where I was."

"Did you see the note? Aunt Jodie's in hospital. Mom's gone to be with her. Said not to worry."

"Saw it last night. Thanks. Gotta get down to check on the dam. Junior'll need help if something's happened."

He left.

Stanton's phone started ringing again.

He grabbed it. "Jess?"

"It's her grandmother. Jessica's disappeared. She must have taken off in the night. She was sleeping right next to me and I didn't hear a thing. The boat's gone. She must have taken it. I thought she might be with you."

"No."

"Or on the way to see you."

"I'll check. Don't worry."

As he left the hotel he remembered Callie saying she and her EcoAction friends were taking the early bus.

Maybe Jessica had gone to say another goodbye. His father had taken the car so Stanton jogged to the campground just outside town.

It was deserted. There was no sign anyone had ever camped there: no beaten-down grass where tents had been pitched, no remnants of fires, no garbage. It was as if the EcoAction band had never been in town, as if they never existed.

Two police cars with lights flashing but no sirens approached. He hid behind a tree, afraid his presence at the campsite would invite suspicion. He didn't want to be held up while police questioned him.

The cars pulled into the campground. Four officers got out and swept the field with flashlights. Stanton pressed himself against the tree.

One of the officers said, "They've taken off."

Another, "They won't get far. We've already got traffic checks on all the roads out of town."

They returned to their cars and pulled out.

Stanton slipped away and jogged back through town, heading for the lake road, hoping he'd find Jessica walking to town. No disappearance, no mystery; she'd simply taken the boat to the slip because she wanted to see him and couldn't wait until morning.

No.

Jessica wouldn't do that. She wouldn't leave her grandmother with the flood coming.

So where was she?

His route took him down Main Street. Les Cuff passed him, driving fast. He turned into Mill Street, tires squealing. Verna Mullen and two town councillors talked quietly at the door of the community hall while behind them half a dozen refugees from the flood, blankets wrapped around their shoulders, peered past them. The lights were on in Carmichael's and a sign on the sidewalk stated *Free breakfast for flood victims.*

Suddenly Stanton wanted to talk to his father, tell him about Jessica, ask him what he should do, where might she have gone. Had he heard from Mom? How was Aunt Jodie? And how was he himself coping with all this trouble? Stanton felt suddenly small and alone, overwhelmed, his mother away and his father preoccupied and their home cut off by floodwater and Jessica taken off without a word. He felt himself swept along by events he didn't understand and couldn't control. He wanted the adults to fix everything, restore normality.

A police cruiser was parked across the entrance to Black River Power, two more inside. The gates still lay where they'd been left after the demonstration, twisted and half wrenched from their supports. The two Black River fire trucks and one from neighbouring Big Pond were parked in the mill yard. Todd, Charlie, and Adam stood by the river where the dam had been. A couple of dozen people stood outside the gates, peering across the yard, talking in hushed voices as if they were in church. His father was standing on the steps to the office with Junior, Les, Sergeant Munn, and two police officers Stanton didn't recognize.

He walked past Black River Power to where Mill Street ended at the river. A small crowd there, too, talking in quiet voices as they watched the torrent of water sluicing over the falls. All that remained of the dam were the massive concrete pillars on each side of the river to which the two outermost cradles had been anchored. The intervening stanchions were gone, the three iron cradles and their logs with them.

A woman muttered over and over, to anyone who'd listen, "Someone did us a favour."

He hurried back up Mill Street, saw his father still busy, walked on to Main, crossed the green, and hurried along Riverside Drive.

Tess and her parents stood in a silent group on the side-walk in front of their house, watching the river recede across the road. Tess ran to him and put her hand on his arm. "Was it a bomb?" she asked.

"Don't know."

"Was your dad there? Is he all right?"

He nodded.

A neighbour joined them. "Is it terrorists? Will they blow up something else?'

"Don't know."

Stanton stood with them, watching the roiling river. Parts of a dock raced past. The heavy timbers of a wharf. A white-and-green couch cushion. A set of wooden steps.

He hurried on to the lake, hoping to encounter Jessica coming from it. The water level had dropped and the boat ramp was already almost completely exposed. The current swirled towards the channel where the lake ran into the river. A young birch tree was swept past, fol-lowed by two garden chairs and a child's plastic climbing frame.

How could an aluminum boat with a ten-horsepower motor resist getting caught up in that roaring current?

The post beside the ramp where Jessica liked to tie the boat was also exposed, but there was no boat there. He peered into the gloom of the lake. No sign of a boat, but he couldn't see far. The eastern sky was just getting light. He thought of calling Mrs. Caithness but had nothing to report except that there was no sign of Jessica or the boat. He sat at the end of the ramp as the sky lightened and stared across the lake.

At 5:30 A.M. he saw something: a silver-grey shape against the lightening gloom of the water. He fixed his eyes on it until it was light enough to see it was a boat. It was too far away to make out if it was Mrs. Caithness's boat, although it looked like it.

No sign of someone at the tiller.

Stanton pictured the boat pitching and bucking in the current, Jessica untying it, then slipping in the darkness as she made her way to the stern to start the motor. Maybe her head slammed against the side of the boat, knocking her unconscious, and the current swept the boat out into the lake. Was she lying in it, still unconscious, or injured and unable to move, while the boat was carried towards where the lake ran into the river, to be swept downriver, over the falls, and into the gorge?

He should call Jessica's grandmother, but she'd be frantic and he didn't know what to say. He called his father but, as he expected, there was no answer. He'd be busy with Sergeant Munn and the other officers. He tried the Black River Power number but also no answer. He thought of calling 911 but there was only one marine search and rescue unit in the province and that was based in Port Carleton. It would be at least two hours, probably three, before it reached Black River.

He jogged back to the mill. It was light now, the sun just rising. The door to the office was closed. The police at the gates stopped him and said no one was allowed in, there'd been an accident, but when he said Willis Frame was his father, he had to see him and Sergeant Munn urgently, someone was missing, maybe adrift on the lake, one of the officers accompanied him and knocked on the door of the office. Sergeant Munn opened it.

Stanton's father, standing behind Sergeant Munn with Les and Junior, said, "Stanton, what's up?"

"Jessica's missing. She took the boat. It's on the lake—I can see a boat and I think it's her grandmother's, but I can't see her so either she's lying in it, maybe injured, or...."

Les said, "Me and Charlie'll take a boat out there."

Stanton's father said, "Tell Todd and Adam to put a boat in here, too, go a bit upriver, stop Jessica's boat if it comes down before it...you know."

Sergeant Munn said, "Is Mrs. Caithness at the cabin?"

Stanton nodded.

Sergeant Munn summoned one of the officers from the gates and said, "Call Search and Rescue and tell 'em we have a—" he stopped and glanced at Stanton. "—A gal missing on the lake. And I want a woman constable at Mrs. Caithness's. Tell her to get to the boat ramp now, fast, and Les Cuff will take her out to the cabin. Okay, Les?"

Les Cuff, already halfway out the door and beckoning to the dam crew, said, "Right."

Sergeant Munn told Stanton, "You look all tuckered out. Sit yourself down."

"I have to get out to the lake."

"Best to wait here."

"No."

"Yes. Really. Les will send word as soon as he has any news."

Stanton sat at his father's desk. His father stood behind him with his hands on his shoulders, squeezing them and patting them from time to time. Sergeant Munn left to confer with the police outside while Junior ran across to Black River Java. He returned with a coffee and two bagels for Stanton. "Tess says you like these."

Stanton was surprised Tess had abandoned her parents to go to work. He suspected it was her way of trying to return to normal. He could relate.

As he reached for the coffee he found his hand was shaking so much he was afraid he'd spill it and Junior said, "Easy, son. Everything's going to be all right."

Sergeant Munn returned and sat at the desk opposite Stanton and asked, "When did you last see Jess?"

"Last night, after the—you know—the demonstration."

"Where was she?"

"At the lake. She was heading to the cabin in the boat."

"And you're certain she got there?"

Stanton nodded. "Mrs. Caithness said she left in the night but she didn't hear her."

"Where were her friends from EcoAction? Might she have gone to visit them?"

"I thought of that. I went to the campsite looking for her. But they're gone."

"Is there any chance she went with them?"

"Don't think so. No. She said goodbye to them after the demonstration, like she wasn't going to see them again."

"Where did she say goodbye to them?"

"Behind Black River Java. I was with her."

"And that was the last you saw of them?"

"Yeah."

"But you don't know if Jessica saw them again."

"Don't know how she could have done."

"But it's possible, eh?"

"I guess so. But it'd have to have been sometime in the night because we were together the whole time until she left in the boat."

Stanton gradually realized Sergeant Munn had crossed some sort of line. He was no longer questioning him about Jessica, seeking information to help find her, out of concern for her safety. He was also questioning him out of suspicion that she'd been involved with the EcoAction band in sabotaging the dam.

Stanton said, "She's just disappeared—right? Who knows why she went out in the boat in the middle of the night?" His voice rose. "Why would she have gone back to the cabin if she was going to hook up with the EcoAction guys?"

"Okay. Sorry."

They sat in silence. Stanton sipped his coffee. He hadn't touched the bagels.

His father's cell rang. He looked at Sergeant Munn, who said, "Answer it."

Stanton's father listened and said, "Okay, Les. Thanks." He shut the phone off.

Stanton thought, *In a second or two, Dad's going to say Jessica's in the boat, I just couldn't see her, and all this is some kind of mix-up. Everything with her and me will be back to normal, the same as always.*

Or he's going to say Jessica's not in the boat, and everything will be different. Forever.

Stanton's father looked at him. "Les found the boat. Jessica's not in it. He has the boat in tow. He's…he's searching the lake."

"I want to go with him."

"Not a good idea."

"Your dad's right," said Sergeant Munn.

Stanton said firmly, "I want to go."

Sergeant Munn looked at Stanton's father, who shrugged and said, "Only if I come with you."

Stanton shook his head. "I'll be okay. And you've got stuff to do here."

"I'll get Les to meet you at the boat launch," said Sergeant Munn. He opened the door and called to one of the officers, "Take Stanton out to the lake."

Les and Charlie were waiting at the boat launch. They'd tied Jessica's boat beside it.

As Stanton climbed in, Les said, "Sure you want to do this?"

"No. But I've got to."

"Worse comes to worst..." said Les carefully, "it won't be pretty."

Stanton tried not to think about it. He sat beside Charlie and asked, "Where do we start?"

Les, at the tiller, said, "Where the lake runs out into the river. Then we work our way around the lake, against the current, until Search and Rescue arrive and take over."

"Have you done this before?"

Les looked at Charlie, said slowly, "Me and Charlie did it once. That was enough."

Charlie, not looking at Stanton, nodded.

Stanton gazed around at the grey immensity of the lake. Eight kilometres long, three kilometres wide, and thirty metres deep in places. Sixteen square kilometres and thousands of gallons of water. What were the chances of finding five-foot-nine, 135-pound Jessica in that? Would they find her floating? Or was she lying at the bottom of the lake, her hair spread and waving like seaweed, eels and catfish and carp swimming around her?

He remembered imagining himself trapped in the car, drowning, when he was driving through the flood. Now that seemed self-indulgent, self-dramatizing. This was real. He didn't know how or what he should feel, fear or grief or anticipation. At that moment, beginning the search, he didn't think he was feeling anything. There was room only for action, for searching, all feelings suspended.

Les said, "Let's go then."

He swung the boat around and headed for where the lake poured into the river.

SIXTEEN

Jessica had a new identity. She was a Missing Person.

Stanton had a new identity, too. Boyfriend of a Missing Person. But what kind of grief did that qualify him for? Not the anguish he'd experienced at a brief meeting with Jessica's parents, called back from their wintering in Florida. Not the fathomless sadness of her grandmother, who sat on the rocks outside the cabin for hours, looking across the lake as if she expected Jessica to rise from the waters at any moment. Not the hysterical weeping that sent girls whom Stanton was sure hardly knew her stumbling to the specially provided grief counsellors at school. He despised the slathering emotion of her girlfriends as they collapsed against him, professing their undying affection for Jessica and promising never, ever to forget her. He couldn't stand the awkward, manly slaps on the shoulder from the boys, her friends and his, all of them, he suspected, secretly jealous of his so effortlessly becoming the centre of attention. He hated the growing heap of stuffed toys left by her locker and by the road at the boat slip. She'd never owned a stuffed toy in her life that he knew of. Why should they be inflicted on her now, in token of what everyone seemed increasingly to assume was her drowning?

He felt himself a kind of grief outcast, didn't know where he belonged in the emotional turmoil that swirled around him wherever he went; not family, not just a friend, somewhere in the middle, where he didn't know what an appropriate expression of grief looked like.

If it even was grief. He wasn't sure what he was feeling, still trapped in the kind of suspension of reality, and with it the suspension of feeling, he'd experienced when he and Les and Charlie were searching the lake, and later watching with Mrs. Caithness while the Search and Rescue team methodically crisscrossed the water. What good did all the grief do, anyway? If you grieved for a missing person, what kind of outpouring of sorrow did you move on to if—when—that person turned up drowned, permanently missing?

Stanton and his father had checked out of the hotel and moved back to their house on Monday, three days after the explosion. They'd found the house still high and dry on its mound, the river almost back to its normal course. Debris was strewn across the driveway and around the yard, though, along with a couple of trees that had been completely uprooted in the flood. Dozens of limbs, boughs, odd lengths of wood from docks, and rocks had washed in.

That same day, the search for Jessica was called off and schools reopened. Stanton went back to class on Tuesday and lasted three hours. He gave up, walked out of second-period English, and went to Black River Java. Tess hugged him and promised, "She'll turn up."

He tried school again on Wednesday, but only lasted one hour. After that, he took to showing up first thing in the morning but leaving before recess. No one in administration said anything; he guessed they didn't dare.

Secretly and guiltily, he was surprised by how little he cared. His father, and his mother on the phone from Aunt Jodie's, kept asking if he was all right, if he needed to talk, and seemed relieved when he said, truthfully, he was fine.

. But missing Jessica was a slow drip of sorrow.

On the Thursday after the explosion, he woke early and walked to the lake and turned to point out to her the way the early morning sun shimmered here and there on the water as it pierced the thinning mist. But she wasn't there.

Drip.

Later the same day he went to Black River Java and bought two coffees and Tess started to say something but stopped and served him both coffees and he carried them to their table by the window and only then remembered she wasn't there.

Drip.

He walked across the green and reached for her hand.

Drip.

Getting dressed on Friday, one week after the night Jessica disappeared, he pulled on a sweater she liked to borrow and caught the lingering smell of her.

Drip.

On the same day Frank Reed came down from the capital to talk to Stanton's father, who had been home all week. TransNational had suspended him while they conducted their own investigation into the destruction of the dam. Reed had called to tell him the morning after the explosion and to say he'd be down to talk to him in a few days.

"But there'll be no one on duty at the mill," Stanton's father had protested.

"Junior will cover for you," said Reed.

"They've made him manager, haven't they?"

Reed hesitated. "Acting manager."

"So he's got what he wanted."

Stanton and his father were setting the house to rights after his mother's flood preparations when Reed arrived on Friday afternoon. Stanton said he'd go to his room but his father said he may as well hear what Mr. Reed had to say, as it would affect the whole family.

"So what's going on?" Stanton's father asked.

"The company feels it would be best for you to take a little time off, after the stress of the last few weeks, and until it's completed its investigation," said Reed.

"I'm a suspect," Stanton's father said. It wasn't a question.

"A *possible* suspect."

"What the hell does that mean?"

"It simply means they want to explore everything leading up to the incident and everyone's role in it, including yours. They know you had access to dynamite on-site and are trained in its use, so of course they have to eliminate the possibility you accessed and used the company's explosives. They know as well as I do it's ridiculous."

"Well, that's something," Stanton's father said. "Plus you and I and Sergeant Munn went to the shed right after the explosion and made sure it hadn't been broken into and checked the store against inventory and confirmed nothing was missing."

"Correct," said Reed. "But there's still the possibility—forgive me saying this, Willis, and it's not coming from me but from head office—there's the possibility of records being falsified and they have to check that out simply to eliminate it as a possibility. I've already told them it's absurd."

"Well, gee, thanks," Stanton's father put in.

"But even when that possibility is eliminated, as you and I know it will be, what cannot be eliminated is your knowledge of explosives, and your ability, if you somehow acquired them elsewhere, to easily dynamite the dam."

"Why don't they just hang me?"

Reed went on carefully. "They also know you're not totally happy in the job, Willis, haven't been for a while, and that you've been critical of the company."

"Nothing I haven't said to their faces."

"And they feel you weren't sufficiently—er—vocal in your support of the company against its critics during the lead-up to the incident."

"During the lead-up to the near flood, you mean. The flood that would have happened if someone hadn't had the courage to save the town from it."

"That's exactly the kind of talk the company doesn't like," Reed warned. "And how can you say that, as if it's a good thing the dam's gone? We're losing thousands of kilowatts of power every day because of it. And you know how the province is compensating for that loss? By firing up the old Ship's Cove Generating Station. That's right. We're heating our homes with oil-fired power instead of hydroelectric power. We've exchanged clean, environmentally friendly power for so-called dirty power. You can talk all you like about how TransNational was spoiling the environment by raising river and lake levels, but now we've got Ship's Cove burning millions of barrels of oil while it spews out around 750 tons per gigawatt hour of greenhouse gases, which makes it one of the single largest sources of air pollution and greenhouse gas in Canada. I wonder if that ever crossed the minds of the EcoAction gang."

"I'm not going to disagree with you," Stanton's father said. "I've worked for Black River Power and TransNational all these years because I believe in hydroelectric power. But I still think TransNational could be—could have been—more sensitive to the town's concerns about water levels."

"I understand and appreciate that, Willis. Everyone at head office feels the same and promises to do better in the future at staying in touch with how the townspeople feel."

"But they still want to get rid of me."

"That's going to be up to you, old friend. They can't fire you without cause. So don't give them one." He shook hands with Stanton's father as he added, "It's all bullshit, all the company's accusations and suspicions. It's just a process they have to go through and it'll blow over in a week or two. But in the meantime, it's what the head guys want."

After Frank Reed's visit, Stanton drove to Black River Java. The town wore a subdued air, like it had immediately after the explosion. He paused at the café door to look down Mill Street at the river and what was left of the dam. Although the current was still strong and fast, the river had dropped to its normal level. Not the normal level established by TransNational Power, but its old normal level, which the townspeople were pleased to point out over and over again.

Tess joined him at the table by the window and looked at him, eyebrows raised in an unspoken question.

He shook his head. "No news."

She put her hand over his where it rested on the table. "No news can be good news."

He shrugged.

She looked around the empty café and sighed. "Do you suppose things will ever be normal again? Like—people coming in for a coffee?"

He shrugged again and she went on, "It's like the whole town's in mourning. But what for? It's surely not for the dam, because most everyone wanted it gone, and it can't be for poor Jessica because she's a Missing Person, not a—" She broke off.

Stanton supplied, "Not a drowned person."

"Sorry. Mom always says my mouth's ahead of my brain," she mumbled.

"It's okay."

A car pulled up at the drive-through window and she went to serve it. When she returned she said, "It's like people are afraid."

"Of what?" Stanton asked.

Tess leaned towards him and lowered her voice. "Of the fact that the crazy person who blew up the dam is still out there."

He'd fallen into the habit of sandwiching afternoon visits to Black River Java between visits to Mrs. Caithness's cabin, where he cleared debris washed up by the flood and carried furniture down from the loft and helped return the cabin to normal. During his first visit, Fred Shingles came over and asked Mrs. Caithness gruffly about Jessica.

Mrs. Caithness said, "Still nothing to report, Fred. Thanks for asking."

He lingered in the doorway and added, "And thanks for...you know."

"I keep telling you, Fred. No need to thank me," she said as she ushered him out of the door.

Seeing Stanton looking at her curiously, she explained, "Sergeant Munn arrested poor Fred right after the explosion, but had to let him go when I told him he'd spent the night here. I told him Fred called in late, after Jessica came in, and I said have a drink and a chat, so he stayed for a drink and talked to Jessica and me, his usual silly nonsense. After a few more drinks he fell asleep, or passed out, one or the other.

"We left him sleeping downstairs, thinking it'd be easier than waking him, and if the flood came he'd wake soon enough, and Jessica and me went up to the loft. He woke me twice in the night, first time shouting something about the sea going to take over the land. I think he was dreaming because he fell to snoring a few seconds later. Second time when he made a racket going outside to pee. I wish I'd checked on Jessica then. I don't know whether or not she was there—right beside me!—and Fred doesn't remember seeing her leave the cabin, but like he said in the morning he was in no state to notice anything."

The next time Stanton visited they had tea and looked out at the lake when they'd finished work and she repeated the account. It was so pat, word for word so much the same both times she told it, Stanton thought she might be lying about Shingles being there all night. He waited for Mrs. Caithness to say something about Jessica, but she didn't, so he ventured, not believing himself, "I'm sure Jessica's all right. Just took off somewhere."

"Oh yes," said Mrs. Caithness, so confidently, and in such contrast to her impenetrable silence immediately after Jessica disappeared, that Stanton wondered if she'd heard from her.

Sergeant Munn came out to the lake on Saturday while Stanton was at the cabin and Shingles was visiting again. Mrs. Caithness greeted him with, "I haven't heard anything from her."

"I know," said Sergeant Munn. "You would have told me if you had, like I asked you to. I just called in to see how you were doing, but I see you already have plenty of help and company."

Shingles set off across the bluff towards his cabin, but Sergeant Munn called, "Hang around a moment, Fred. I need to talk to you."

"Now what?" Shingles demanded.

"Just something I heard in town. Can we talk in private?"

"No. 'Cause then you can accuse me of saying something I never said. Anything you got to say you can say right here, in front of witnesses."

Sergeant Munn sighed. "Okay, Fred, as you wish. There's a rumour going around town of a white-haired male being seen on Main Street around two in the morning on the night the dam blew. Turns out a woman staying at the shelter couldn't sleep and went outside for a smoke and saw this white-haired individual lurking—that was the word the lady used—lurking near the intersection with Mill Street."

Shingles stalked back across the rocks and thrust his face close to Sergeant Munn's. "A white-haired man. Not many of them around, are there? And the shelter's only—what? —a couple hundred metres from the intersection, and it was dark that night, so your informant would have had a really clear view of this white-haired man—"

"That'll do with the sarcasm, Fred," said Sergeant Munn. "I'm just telling you what has been reported to me, and what I'm obliged to investigate."

"You can investigate all you like but it's still got nothing to do with me."

"So I have to ask you again, if you don't mind—"

"I do."

"Where were you on the night the dam blew?"

Shingles rolled his eyes. "Like I've told you and your cronies a few dozen times already and like Mrs. Caithness has told you too, I was right here at the lake all that night and I wish you'd stop harassing a respectable senior citizen."

Sergeant Munn turned to Mrs. Caithness. "Forgive my having to ask again, Lily."

"Yes, Ernie, he was here, passed out and snoring like an elephant," said Mrs. Caithness.

Sergeant Munn turned back to Shingles. "I'll be talking to you again, Fred, so don't go anywhere, please."

"Like where?" said Shingles.

"Like over the border," said Sergeant Munn.

Stanton had expected his father to fall into some kind of depression after Frank Reed's visit, but instead he'd set straight to work clearing the yard and the meadows around their house of debris washed there by the overflowing river. He cut the wood into chunks and stacked them to use in the wood stove, raked the gravel that had been washed into the meadows, and carted it back to the driveway to spread. He talked of ploughing up part of the meadows and planting vegetables in the spring to sell at the farmers' markets, maybe supplying the SaveEasy and Foodmart. Taking advantage, he said, of the growing demand for locally grown food, and never returning to TransNational, even if they wanted him back.

"Go for it," said Stanton.

"It'd be just a part-time thing, at least to start with," said his father. "I'd have to get another job to keep enough money coming in."

"Enough for what?"

"Well, you know, enough to live on."

"You mean for me to get through university."

"That, too."

"Just be a farmer, if that's what you want," said Stanton. "I can get a loan, even a scholarship if I'm lucky."

Stanton's mother telephoned every day. In her latest call she said Aunt Jodie was out of hospital and recovering at home. "But don't call me," she added. "She's sleeping a lot and I don't want the phone to wake her."

"I'll tell Dad," said Stanton. "He's out in the yard, clearing up. I'm helping him. Just came in to make some tea."

"I hope you boys are all right," said his mother. "I'm so torn between wanting to be home with both of you with your troubles and worries, and wanting to stay with Jodie."

"It's okay, Mom, really. Dad and I have each other for company and she's got no one else."

SEVENTEEN

On Sunday, nine days after the explosion, Sergeant Munn paid a visit to Stanton's place. He asked Stanton how he was he holding up and if he had heard from Jessica. Then he asked if Stanton and his father would mind answering a few questions. It was something he had to do, he explained, in order to "dot all the i's and cross all the t's" before the heavy-duty anti-terrorist guys took over the investigation, which he knew they were about to do. The more information he could give them, he said, the better it would be for Willis and Stanton.

Stanton's father said, "Fire away."

Sergeant Munn took out a notebook and asked Stanton, "Do you have any idea where your EcoAction friends might have gone? All my calls to their headquarters in BC get forwarded to a smart-arse lawyer in New York who says he's never heard of Callie Jost or Brynne Tanner."

"They're not my friends. I only met them through Jessica."

"Was Jess with them on Friday night after the demonstration?"

"They went to the campground, and she went to her grandmother's. I took her to the lake. I told you."

"Did she come back and join them?"

"Not as far as I know. I told you that, too."

"After you left her at the boat slip and she went out to her gran's, did she come back to town and spend the night with you?"

Stanton felt himself colouring. He glanced at his father. "No!"

"Reason I ask is—if she did, I'd know she had nothing to do with the explosion, her having been with you all night, and you confirming that."

So Jessica, along with Callie and Brynne, was a suspect until Sergeant Munn had proof of her whereabouts through the night of the explosion. Stanton thought about lying, swearing she was with him all night, but repeated firmly, his voice louder, "I took her to the lake. I watched her set off for the cabin. She was in the boat. The one Mr. Cuff and Mr. Hatt found without her in it. All right?"

Sergeant Munn raised his hands as if to shield himself from Stanton's retort. "I'm sorry. It's just that I have to be sure about every detail."

Stanton muttered, "Okay."

"So what time did you get back to the hotel after you left Jess at the lake?"

"About eight o'clock."

"And then you stayed there all night?"

Stanton nodded.

"Did anyone see you come in?"

"Don't think so. No one was at the desk."

Stanton realized Sergeant Munn had moved stealthily from asking about Jessica's movements on Friday night to asking about his own movements. Did that mean he was a suspect, too?

"Was your dad at the hotel?"

"No. I watched TV for a bit, then left him a note about Mom and fell asleep."

"What about your mom?"

"Just she went to Lewisport to see her sister in hospital."

Sergeant Munn looked at Stanton's father. "Jodie's in hospital? Anything serious?"

"The usual. Don't know how bad yet."

"Send her my best," said Sergeant Munn. "Never rains but it pours, eh?"

Stanton's father nodded.

Sergeant Munn asked Stanton, "Did you see your dad any time in the night?"

Stanton thought back to Friday night. The explosion had woken him, he was sure of that, but when his father appeared seconds later he was already dressed. He'd gone out and had returned to the room to tell Stanton he thought he'd heard an explosion and it sounded like it was maybe at the dam. It was almost like he was dressed and ready for it. Almost like he knew it was coming.

"Not 'til around three. I think the explosion woke me."

Stanton's father said, "Hold it, Ernie. I told you all this right after the explosion. I left the mill around eleven Friday night, walked back to the hotel, so got there just after eleven, and was there until around three."

"I thought you had supper with Frank."

"I went back to the mill after we had supper. We called ahead to Mario's Pizza out on the highway because nothing was open in town. We were only gone for a half hour. Junior stayed at the mill. Frank went straight home. I brought Junior back a slice of pizza. I told you that, too."

"And then you went to the hotel and were there all night."

"With Stanton."

"In the same room?"

"No. But dammit, Ernie. Where the hell else do you think I was if I wasn't at the hotel?"

"Sorry, Willis. I just need you to confirm you weren't back at the mill until after three."

"You know I wasn't."

"It's just that Junior saw a light-coloured car parked at the end of Mill Street, down by the river, when he ran across to Black River Java to get a coffee just before three. He couldn't see the registration plate and didn't take any notice, anyway, thinking it was a couple parked down there, the way they do sometimes. He said he talked to Tess for maybe a minute, so was away from the office for no more than three or four minutes. The car was gone when he came back.

"I spoke to Tess and she said they talked for more like five minutes, which means he was away from the mill for close to ten minutes. Long enough for someone who knew what he—or she…"—Sergeant Munn paused and looked at Stanton—"…was doing to slip in, set a charge or two, and get out. Junior said the car was definitely gone when he returned. Tess saw it, too, and described it the same way: light, she thought maybe yellow, with something on the side—some kind of design or decoration; maybe flowers—but it was dark and she couldn't see much, including the registration plate."

He looked at Stanton's father. "What colour is your car, Willis? Just for the record."

"Light green. You know that, too."

"You have access to explosives—right?"

"Of course. They're for ice jams and are kept in the storage shed. Always padlocked. Still padlocked."

"Anyone else have access?"

"Only other person who has authorized access is Junior but he still has to get the key from me."

"And no explosives are missing."

"You were with Frank Reed and me when we checked."

Sergeant Munn turned to a new page in his notebook. "Your turn, Stanton. Just one more thing and we're done. You went to Home Hardware last Friday."

Stanton felt his face heating up again. He tried to fight it down, aware Sergeant Munn was watching him closely. "Yeah."

"What did you get there?"

"Just some stuff."

He recalled Sergeant Munn watching when he left the town meeting with Jessica and Callie and Brynne to reconnoitre the mill, and when they all went to Black River Java the next day. He'd thought Sergeant Munn was watching the EcoAction people. He must have been watching him, too. He was glad he'd deleted the pages of the EcoAction manual from his cellphone. He suspected Sergeant Munn could have someone retrieve them, in which case he'd have to pretend he'd lost his phone. He prepared to say that but Sergeant Munn went on.

"Have you still got this stuff?"

"Yeah."

"May I see it, please?"

Stanton retrieved his purchases from under the bed in his room and laid them out on the kitchen table.

"What the hell is all this?" said his father.

"Looks like some kind of science project," said Sergeant Munn. He looked steadily at Stanton. "And this is everything you bought that day."

Stanton nodded.

"So nothing has been used in any way?"

"Haven't touched the stuff since I bought it. Haven't even looked at it."

He guessed Sergeant Munn had a copy of the receipt. Would he try matching the items on the printout with the items in Stanton's possession? Would he notice if some were missing? Would he believe Stanton if he said he'd lost them on the way back to the hotel? Would it be better to admit he'd tried to make a bomb but got frightened by what he was doing and threw his effort away?

"What were you thinking of making?" Sergeant Munn asked, looking hard at Stanton.

"Nothing," Stanton lied. "Just thought it was stuff that might come in useful around the house."

"As long as that's all it is," said Sergeant Munn. "Maybe you and your father should have a talk about it."

He looked at Stanton's father, who nodded, perplexed. "Sure, but...."

"Stanton will tell you about his—er—project. Won't you, Stanton?"

Stanton nodded, his head down, avoiding his father's gaze.

As Sergeant Munn left, he told Stanton, "If you hear from Jessica, you'll let me know right away, please."

"Of course," said Stanton.

Adding silently, *Like hell I will.*

"So what were you going to do with that stuff?" Stanton's father asked when Sergeant Munn had gone. "And why hide it in your room?"

Stanton couldn't decide whether to stick to his lie or tell the truth. He took a deep breath and said quickly, "I was planning on making a bomb to blow up the dam. I found out how to make one from...." He was going to say from Callie and Brynne's EcoAction manual but thought he'd better keep quiet about that. "From the web."

His father stared at him and Stanton blurted, "Keeping the dam closed was wrong and I thought TransNational should be taught a lesson."

He didn't mention that he also hoped it would make him a hero in Jessica's eyes. He was embarrassed not so much by having the stuff as by his failure to use it.

"Jesus Christ," said his father. "Did you?"

"Did I what?"

"Blow up the dam."

"No!"

"Thank God for that."

"You really think I'd do it?"

Although he spoke indignantly, Stanton felt almost proud that his father thought him capable of it.

"Of course not," said his father. He sighed and ran his hand through his hair. "Come here."

Stanton took a step towards his father, who held his arms out to hug him.

Stanton stopped. "Wait. Was it you?"

"That blew up the dam? How could you think that?"

"Because you talked about doing it yourself. You said there's more than one way to open the gates and to keep them open. And you had explosives in the mill yard. What is it they say on the TV cop shows? You had means, motive, and opportunity."

His father laughed. "I guess that's what Ernie's thinking. Why he keeps questioning me. He's been watching too much TV. I guess we're the same, you and me. All talk. And just talk."

Stanton knew his father never lied to him, and he never lied to his father. Almost never.

The only reason his father would lie to him would be to protect him from something—like a truth that would put Stanton in the uncomfortable position of knowing something he could never reveal, even under intense questioning.

And that was the only reason Stanton would lie to his father. He was sure his father knew that.

His father hugged him and said, "Sorry."

"What for?"

"For putting ideas like that in your head. It was wrong of me. I was just sounding off. I never should have spoken like that in front of you."

"It wasn't just you made me think of blowing up the dam. Callie and Brynne were talking about it. They scoped out the dam. I was with them. They may even be the ones who did it."

"And Jess with them?"

"I don't see how. I saw her set off for her grandma's that night, like I told Sergeant Munn."

"Do you want to tell him about Callie and Brynne checking out the dam?"

"No."

Stanton's father sighed again. "Jesus, you're putting me in a jam."

"Sorry."

"But best we keep quiet about it, eh?"

"I think—yeah."

"That makes us partners in crime. Withholding evidence or whatever they call it. Don't tell your mother. We don't want to make her an accomplice."

"I don't think she'd mind. She was mad at TransNational, too. She said they'd pay—like, she'd make them pay—if they caused another flood."

"Still. Don't tell her. And if Ernie asks more questions, say exactly what you've said so far and no more."

"It's the truth. I don't know for sure that Callie and Brynne did it, or if Jessica was involved."

★★★

The next morning, ten days after the explosion, Stanton answered the phone in the house and his mother said, "Jodie's out of hospital and doing well. I'm here at the bus station. Can you or Willis come and get me?"

"You didn't have to get the bus. One of us could have driven to Lewisport and picked you up."

"I didn't want to bother you and anyway it's not a bad bus ride. Jodie offered to drive me down, but I didn't think she should drive any distance yet."

Stanton and his father went to town to pick her up. On the way home she explained that Jodie had missed the news of the explosion and Jessica's disappearance while she was in hospital. "When she found out she as good as ordered me home, although she still has to take things easy."

The next day a letter arrived from Jessica.

Stanton picked up the mail. He didn't show it to his parents. He had no intention of showing it to Sergeant Munn either, and didn't want his father to feel he had to tell him about it. It was a notecard with a scene of the White Mountains. It was postmarked Vermont but there was no return address on the envelope or inside. Stanton wondered if Jessica thought Sergeant Munn was intercepting his mail, suspecting she hadn't drowned but had taken off with her EcoAction comrades. Were the police allowed to do that? He sat on the bench in front of the post office where the old men sat in summer and read.

> *Dear Stanton,*
> *I'm with an EcoAction cell protesting clear-cutting to make room for a golf course at a ski resort. Callie texted just after 12:00 the night after the demo and*

said we're outta here come with us. They had a car—don't know where they got it—and said they'd pick me up at the lake. I sneaked out of the cabin and took the boat. I was going to leave it by the ramp but the current was so strong it ripped the rope out of my hands and carried the boat away.

I didn't tell you or Grandma because I knew neither of you would want me to go and it would have been too hard explaining. I didn't want to argue in the middle of the night.

We're done here. Moving on today.

Take care,

J

P.S. Love you

He didn't know what he'd expected from her, if anything, but it wasn't a notecard with a pretty picture, as if they were just friends and she was on holiday and would be home soon. He carried it around with him all day and then walked across the meadows and tore it up and threw it in the river.

It didn't help.

Drip.

EIGHTEEN

Six weeks later, Stanton was standing in the front doorway on a Friday morning, watching his father tilling the meadow that lay between the old farmhouse and the river in preparation for planting his market garden in the spring. He'd taken a job as a relief cashier at the credit union in Black River. He didn't like it but said it was a temporary measure to bring in a little extra money until the market garden business was established.

The phone rang and Stanton went back into the house to answer it.

Aunt Jodie said, "Willis or Stanton?"

"Stanton."

"You sound just like your father."

"Everyone says that."

"It's your Aunt Jodie."

"I know."

"How's everything with you, gorgeous boy? How's life in not-so-sleepy Black River since the dam exploded? Is your dad coping okay?"

"He's okay."

"And is there any word on dear Jessica?"

He lied, "No. Not yet."

"Poor boy. Poor girl. But I'm sure there's a simple explanation, and she'll turn up."

He hadn't spoken to Aunt Jodie since she was in hospital.

"How are you? Are you feeling better?"

"Better than what?"

He didn't want Aunt Jodie to go into details about her irritable bowel. It would be just like her to do so.

"Just...better," he said cautiously.

"I have never felt better, dear boy. If I was any better I'd be dangerous. Your mother and I had a lovely time together. We went to every women's clothing store in Lewisport, but don't tell your father, and we went to the movies twice, and we went out to supper at the new Chinese restaurant here, and we walked miles every day. We spent every minute together, just the two of us, like old times."

It didn't sound to Stanton as if Aunt Jodie had been very sick but he decided maybe she was making light of her illness.

"I'm afraid you've missed Mom. She's gone for a walk before she gets down to work," Stanton said.

He thought of the pile of clothing waiting for her attention. She was taking in women's dresses and other garments for alteration and adjustment, to augment the income from her bookkeeping, and the new business had proved unexpectedly popular.

"Never mind," said Aunt Jodie. "Tell her I'm coming down tomorrow so we can visit the Big Pond flea market like we planned when she was here. I hope that'll be okay and if it's not tell her too bad I'm coming anyway and she can't call me because I've lost my cellphone—I'm calling from the café where I'm having breakfast—and I'm working on a mural in that new store that's opening soon in the middle of nowhere between Lewisport and Black River, it's called Rural Delights, you know the one...."

"No."

"Well, you wouldn't, being a man, but anyway I'm paint-
ing murals there all day today and I don't know where I'm
staying tonight but I'll just drive on down to Black River
in the morning."

"Are you sure your old car will make it all the way here?"
Stanton teased.

"Don't start on about my cars, dear boy. I have a new one
anyway. A new old one, that is."

"What make is it?"

"How should I know? And who cares, anyway? I chose
it because it's a nice shade of yellow. I've already painted
some flowers on the side to brighten it up. Anyway, tell your
mom I'll see her soon. Bye, gorgeous boy."

"See ya, Aunt Jodie."

Stanton hung up, grabbed his backpack, and went outside.
He was driving to school today. Something was nagging at
the fringes of his memory as he set off up the driveway but
he dismissed it for now.

He waved to his father in the yard, who paused the
tiller and waved back, grinning. Stanton hadn't seen him
so enthusiastic about work for years. He thought bleakly
that Jessica would at last approve of his father's job if she
knew.

At the end of the driveway he saw his mother approaching,
walking briskly at the side of the road. He stopped, opened
the window, and related the details of Aunt Jodie's call.

"She's coming tomorrow?" his mother asked. "Driving
down?"

"I thought that would be okay."

"Of course it is. I'm just…surprised she's driving so soon.
After her…you know…."

In town, Stanton stopped at Black River Java. He was
going to be late for school anyway, and decided he may as

well miss the first two classes. His marks were fine despite his truancy, and he still seemed to have a free pass in his coming and going; Jessica's disappearance still apparently gave him immunity from any kind of reproach.

The café was quiet and Tess joined him at the table by the window. She seemed to sit a little closer every time he came in. Stanton was ambivalent: he didn't really care whether she sat beside him or on the other side of the room.

He'd twice given in to the badgering of his friends to hang out as a group. The first time they went to a movie, the second time to a concert. Both times, Stanton had to sidestep the advances of a couple of Jessica's friends. His status as a tragic figure seemed to make him a target. As the group walked home from the concert, Erica moved in and kissed him before he could withdraw. He felt such a rush of loss and longing for Jessica that he backed away in revulsion. He apologized awkwardly and tried to laugh it off by pretending he had thought he was going to sneeze.

As he left the coffee shop, Les, Todd, Charlie, and Adam arrived. They nodded but didn't speak. Stanton thought they held him partly responsible for the destruction of the dam, through his association with Jessica, since she had brought the EcoAction protestors to town, and the mill workers believed they were the perpetrators. Everyone except Junior had been laid off. TransNational had offered them work in the capital but they declined and said they'd wait for the dam to be rebuilt and Black River Power to resume operation. Tess said Les Cuff talked about it being a bleak Christmas for the kids this year.

Outside, Stanton glanced towards Mill Street. Something was still on his mind, something Aunt Jodie said about her new car.

He pushed it aside when he saw Junior making his way slowly towards Black River Java. He saw Stanton and lifted his hand in a wary greeting. Stanton nodded in return. They hadn't really spoken since their skirmish at the mill and Stanton wasn't about to start now. Junior was still acting manager but had nothing to manage. The gates at the mill hung open like they always had, and people wandered in and across the yard with their Black River Java coffee and watched the river flowing fast and smooth towards its tumble down the gorge.

Verna Mullen, with the support of Blaine Tupper, talked of the dam being rebuilt, as TransNational planned, but there was strong opposition in the town and the council was divided. Meanwhile Ship's Cove Generating Station continued to make up the power lost by the destruction of the Black River dam and had so far emitted over half a million tons of greenhouse gases, at Stanton's last count.

★★★

Stanton went to his math class and language arts, and then went out to the lake to see Mrs. Caithness, whom he still visited at least twice a week.

Fred Shingles often visited, too, although now, according to Mrs. Caithness, he was somewhere in the southern states. Stanton didn't know whether Sergeant Munn had lifted the ban on his crossing the border or if Shingles had somehow sneaked across. He'd told Mrs. Caithness he was training with an organization called the Sons of Freedom. She didn't believe him, and thought he was staying in a Florida condo with a brother he sometimes spoke of.

When Stanton arrived, happy to get away from school, he found Mrs. Caithness in front of the cabin, sitting on the rocks despite the cold of mid-December. He sat with her and they watched the lake, now at the level it was when she and her husband had first moved there. They talked of where Jessica might be and what she might be doing.

She'd telephoned twice to assure her grandmother she was well and happy but didn't say where she was. Stanton suspected it was because she was still a Person of Interest to the team of hard-eyed investigators who had swarmed the town in search of terrorists after the explosion, questioning all those already questioned by Sergeant Munn and Constable Dave, receiving all answers with expressionless scepticism. Stanton wouldn't put it past them to tap Mrs. Caithness's phone and suspected Jessica and her grandmother were wary of the same thing.

He followed EcoAction's campaigns on the organization's website and pictured Jessica involved in all of them: marching in New York to protest inaction over climate change, standing in a line of protesters on Vancouver Island to stop the advance of clear-cutting equipment, sitting with residents of a village in Argentina to protest open-pit gold mining, being threatened by soldiers in Tanzania in a demonstration against the use of child labourers in gold mines. He imagined her standing before a crowd of protesters, inciting them to action, one arm in the air, fist clenched, the way she'd stood beside Brynne at the meeting in Black River. She'd wear a red beret and her hair would be unruly, less sleek than it used to be, and her complexion would be coarsened by long hours demonstrating in the open air.

He felt a kind of pride in her, comparing her courage and commitment, her willingness to take action, with his own reluctance to use his bomb-making equipment, and his timid and surreptitious disposal of his failed attempt in the garbage before his mother or father found it and asked awkward questions.

He hadn't heard from her, apart from the solitary, dismissive-seeming postcard. If she sent another, he wouldn't tear it up and throw it in the river. He wished he still had the one she sent. He wondered if she ever thought of him.

He feared not.

Mrs. Caithness made tea and they drank it at the table inside. She'd started a blog and she read him her latest entry.

> *I've always loved how the lake changes as fall advances towards winter. The reeds and cattails and duckweed are dying back. The herons and osprey are departing for southern coastlines, although a few black and eider ducks still hang around. The northern harriers cruise the last low growing vegetation at the lake's edge, while the bald eagles patrol as watchfully as ever. Soon they, my neighbour, and I will be left alone at the lake, its solitary guardians until spring.*

She looked up. "I hope Jessica finds the blog, wherever she is. We both always liked how the lake changes through the year. This way, if she reads it, we can still enjoy the changing seasons together. It would be like she's still here with me."

When he rose to leave he asked, as he always did, "Are you managing okay? Is there anything I can do?"

Jessica's grandmother said, as always, "I'm fine, thank you, dear."

NINETEEN

The next morning Aunt Jodie arrived. She jumped out of her car in a whirl of chiffon and hugged first her sister, then Stanton's father, and then Stanton.

She said, giggling, "You'll never guess what happened. I was stopped for speeding on my way through town and the charming young officer, he said his name was Dave Watson, was very interested in my car, and wanted to know all about it—and about me! Where I lived, had I driven the car in Black River recently, did I let anyone else drive it." She shook her head, smiling. "I said no and he said had anyone borrowed it recently and I said well just my sister a few weeks ago and he asked who was that and where did she live and I said Angie Frame of Black River and he seemed surprised. Then he asked where was I going and let me off with a warning about speeding and sent me on my way. Now what do you suppose that was all about?"

Stanton and his father stared at the light yellow car, at the flowers painted on the sides. Stanton's father shifted his eyes to the road. Stanton followed his gaze.

Another car was approaching: a police cruiser with Sergeant Munn at the wheel.

Stanton's mother saw the car, too.

Stanton's father started, "How—"

"Fred provided everything," Stanton's mother said; she was talking fast. "He was going to do it himself but I told him he was already under suspicion and the police were probably watching him after what he said at the meeting. He told me where to put the explosives and showed me how to set the charge so I'd have a few seconds to get clear."

"But Aunt Jodie said you were together all the time you were away," said Stanton.

"We were, except for one night when I said I wanted to visit an old friend who was sick with the flu and I said you shouldn't come, Jodie, because you had yoga and there was no need for you to miss it."

"That night you borrowed my car," said Aunt Jodie. "So what?"

"Then you were asleep before I got back. I lied. Sorry."

Sergeant Munn was halfway across the meadow.

Stanton's mother rushed on. "I knew Junior always left the office in the early morning to get a coffee when he's on nights, like you do, Willis, and there was no way he'd be back before the dam blew, so there was no danger of anyone getting hurt. I was in and out in a couple of minutes. It was easy."

Sergeant Munn had parked and was approaching.

Aunt Jodie said, "Whatever is going on?"

Stanton's mother hugged her husband, then Stanton, then her sister. She squared her shoulders and turned to face Sergeant Munn with a look of resignation.

Stanton said, "But Mom, why?"

His mother shrugged. "Someone had to do something."

MORE FROM NIMBUS

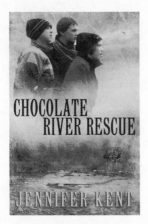

Winner of the
Hackmatack Award
978-1-55109-600-1

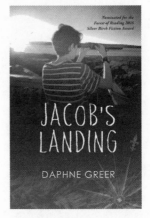

Shortlisted for the
Hackmatack and
Silver Birch Awards
978-1-77108-279-2

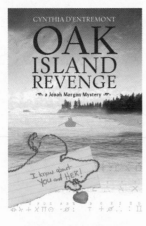

Shortlisted for the
Red Maple Award
978-1-55109-899-9

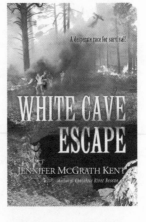

Shortlisted for the
Silver Birch Award
978-1-55109-711-4